The Young Oxford Book of
Mystery Stories

Other Oxford anthologies you might enjoy

The Young Oxford Book of Train Stories
The Young Oxford Book of Sports Stories
The Young Oxford Book of Football Stories
The Young Oxford Book of War Stories

The Young Oxford Book of

MYSTERY STORIES

Dennis Hamley

OXFORD
UNIVERSITY PRESS

OXFORD
UNIVERSITY PRESS

Great Clarendon Street, Oxford OX2 6DP

Oxford University Press is a department of the University of Oxford.
It furthers the University's objective of excellence in research, scholarship,
and education by publishing worldwide in

Oxford New York
Auckland Bangkok Buenos Aires
Cape Town Chennai Dar es Salaam Delhi Hong Kong Istanbul
Karachi Kolkata Kuala Lumpur Madrid Melbourne Mexico City Mumbai
Nairobi São Paulo Shanghai Taipei Tokyo Toronto

Oxford is a registered trade mark of Oxford University Press
in the UK and in certain other countries

This selection and arrangement © Dennis Hamley 2003

The moral rights of the author have been asserted

Database right Oxford University Press (maker)

First published 2003

All rights reserved. No part of this publication may be reproduced,
stored in a retrieval system, or transmitted, in any form or by any means,
without the prior permission in writing of Oxford University Press.
Within the UK, exceptions are allowed in respect of any fair
dealing for the purpose of research or private study, or criticism or
review, as permitted under the Copyright, Designs and Patents Act 1988,
or in the case of reprographic reproduction in accordance with
the terms of the licences issued by the Copyright Licensing Agency.
Enquiries concerning reproduction outside these terms and in other
countries should be sent to the Rights Department, Oxford University Press,
at the above address.

This book is sold subject to the condition that it shall not, by way of trade or
otherwise, be lent, re-sold, hired out or otherwise circulated without
the publisher's prior consent in any form of binding or cover other than that in
which it is published and without a similar condition including this condition
being imposed on the subsequent purchaser.

British Library Cataloguing in Publication Data available

ISBN 0 19 278197 9

1 3 5 7 9 10 8 6 4 2

Typeset by AFS Image Setters Ltd, Glasgow

Printed in Great Britain by
Mackays of Chatham Ltd, Chatham, Kent

For Ella
when she's old enough

Contents

Introduction

Mysteries. What are they? A bit of a mystery really—the word can mean so many things. Which do you prefer? A dead body in a closed room with a host of suspects, the least likely being the murderer? A strange phenomenon which may have a rational solution, maybe a hallucination—or maybe a ghost? Stonehenge or the Statues on Easter Island? What is our Universe? Why are we here? Do we have free will or are we living predestined lives?

Well, they aren't all here in this book—but some are. You'll read a lot of 'Whodunnits?'—some jokey spoofs, some deadly serious—and variations where we don't ask 'whodunnit?' but 'who is going to do it?'. You'll meet the supernatural or magic or—who knows? There's one story set on another planet far in the future—but who's to say that someone today couldn't go through the same mysterious events? And you'll find a story which deals with the biggest mystery of all—or at least how it appears to a ten-year-old boy. I'm not telling you which story is which. You must find out for yourself.

A lot of marvellous authors have written super stories for this collection. I can only thank them for making my task in putting the book together so easy and such a delight. It just shows how asking that first question, 'Mysteries. What are they?' brings out so many different answers, with many writers able to show us exactly what they mean.

Enjoy it. And if you do, please let me know. I've got plenty more here—if you want them!

Dennis Hamley

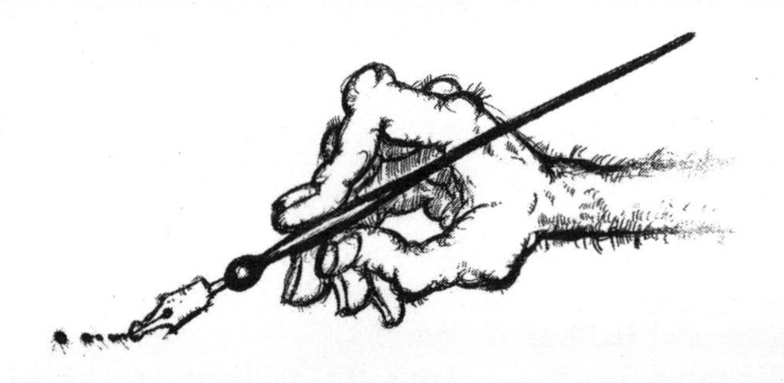

The Adventure of the Dented Computer

SIMON CHESHIRE

OK. I just have to accept it. I'm borderline genius.

There are any number of clever kids at St Egbert's School, but I can honestly say, without fear of contradiction, that I'm right up there at the top of the food chain.

My name is Sherlock Holmes. Well, no, actually my name is Kevin, but I'm giving serious thought to having it legally changed. My mum started whimpering and tugging at her collar when I announced my intention, so I think she's OK about it. She's nearly used to the deerstalker hat now.

And it's a *real* deerstalker! A proper one. Exactly like Sherlock Holmes wears.

It was my grandad's. 'What d'yer want wi' that dusty old thing?' he said when we found it in his attic. It would have been far too long and complicated to start telling him all about the greatest fictional detective of all time, and how I was destined to be his real-life counterpart. Grandad's not too hot on paying attention. So I said it was for a school project, and he smiled happily and patted my head, and all was fine.

Now then. My first case. It was a classic example of deductive reasoning, which I'm sure even Holmes himself would have been proud of. And a right sinister, nefarious, no-good scheme was at the very heart of this strange and baffling mystery!

I'd been on the lookout for a chance to begin my detective career for ages. I'd read all the Holmes stories twice. Except for a couple of the longer ones. And I'd taped the play versions off Radio 4 and listened to them under the bedclothes at night, so I think that counts.

It started first thing on the Monday morning after half term. We'd had to do an essay over the holiday entitled 'An Example of Great Literature'. Naturally, I'd written about *The Hound of the Baskervilles*, Holmes's most famous case. Five hundred words, Mrs Womsey had wanted, and I'd done five hundred and twelve! Wayne Banks did 'Meka-Robots Comic Summer Special'. What a twit. Everyone else did Harry Potter.

Except Thug Robinson. Now, with a nickname like Thug, you can tell he wasn't the sort to go around being nice to small puppies and having tea with the vicar, can't you? He had a scar above his left eye from where he'd fallen off the roof of the toilet block just before Christmas, and if he'd ever bothered to wash his meaty hands you'd have seen the split knuckles he'd got from demanding dinner money with menaces. You didn't want to be in Thug's bad books, unless you enjoyed going to the dentist.

Thug had done *War and Peace*. By some bloke called Toystory, or something.

We all just sat there, silent. Staring at him. I'd seen

that book on the bookshelf at home. I think Mum had got it cheap somewhere. Anyway, it wasn't something you actually *read.* It was huge, with tiny print, boring, boring, historical, Russian, boring.

Thug stood at the front, and read out his essay. And we were entranced. He actually made the whole thing sound great. Mrs Womsey was speechless: 'Oh, that was lovely, Jonathan [Thug's real name, tee hee], lovely. Superb analysis of the book and the author, that really was one of the very best . . . '

And so on. Believe me, for Mrs Womsey, that's speechless.

If it had happened once, me and the rest of 7A might have put it down to luck. Or a sudden attack of intelligence. Or copying it out of an encyclopaedia.

But he did it again on Tuesday, in French. He turned in a perfect translation of a bit in our textbook *France: The Language, The People* that was so covered in squiggly accents it looked as if someone had sneezed ink on it. Ten out of ten for Thug again.

And again on Wednesday. Chemistry. He'd not only done his homework, he'd put a formula for a new type of plastic in the margin that apparently had the Staff Room baffled for nearly a week.

It was getting worrying. Us clever kids were under threat. Well, we were always under threat from Thug Robinson, but we were more used to it being a gimme-your-cash-or-I'll-thump-you type of threat. We weren't used to having our brains challenged.

Time for me, Sherlock, to solve the mystery! I stood on a desk on Thursday breaktime and announced that I would personally get to the bottom of the matter. Once the laughter had subsided, I approached Weasel Watson.

His name really was Watson. So he was destined to

be my sidekick. He had no choice. He was a tall kid, and very thin. Looked like a weasel, moved like a weasel, ate like a horse that's missed its breakfast.

'So,' I concluded, after telling him about my status as the real-life Holmes and his as my personal Dr Watson. 'Are you set for adventure? Are you ready to gasp in disbelief at my powers of detection? Are you set to become my trusty companion in the fight against evil?'

'No.'

I bought him five bars of chocolate and a packet of chicken crisps from the school canteen and he changed his mind.

'Where you going to start?' he said, checking through the change in his pocket to see if he had enough for an ice cream. 'I mean, how do we know he's not just thumping some other kid until they do his homework for him?'

'No, we'd have heard on the grapevine if that was happening. Remember the homework copying scam of 9C? Collapsed in a fortnight. No, he's getting his information from outside the school.'

Watson picked at his teeth. The bell for afternoon lessons would be going any minute. Kids were hurrying up and down the corridor. The swotty ones were hurrying to their classrooms. The rest of them were hurrying as far away from their classrooms as possible.

'Maybe he's just got a really clever dad,' said Watson.

'Have you *seen* his dad?' I said, raising an eyebrow. 'Thug could be his clone. I doubt the man can spell his own name, let alone do a diagram of the human circulation system.'

'Well, maybe he's got a really stupid dad, but a super-fast Internet connection and loads of useful addresses?'

'No! Think, Watson, think. He's answering very specific questions, doing very specific essays. Teachers spot downloaded stuff straight off, even *our* teachers. You'd have to reorganize the information really intelligently if you were going to do that. And there's no way Thug could manage it.'

Watson thought carefully for a few moments. 'I don't get it,' he said at last.

I was delighted. Watson was turning out to be a perfect sidekick.

'Elementary, my dear Watson,' I said. 'We can deduce two important points from what we already know. Point one: Thug is stealing this information. No kid we know could produce homework of this quality. No adult would supply him with it, either willingly or unwillingly. They hate him more than we do. But! Point two: he must be getting the information from a source *connected* to the school, because it matches up so spot-on with the homework we're being set. His source is therefore likely to be someone who *knows* what the questions are in advance.'

Watson's jaw dropped. He really was ideal sidekick material, this kid.

'A teacher?' he gasped.

'That is a distinct possibility,' I said. At this point, Sherlock Holmes would have popped his curly pipe into his mouth and puffed away mysteriously. I'd tried using a cardboard cut-out pipe before, but it didn't look right. I'd decided to ditch the idea. Besides, smoking was a dirty habit and I didn't want to set a bad example for Watson.

The bell went for lessons. During Maths I scribbled a few notes in the back of my exercise book and gave a good think to the problem of what to do next.

Holmes had his Baker Street Irregulars, so I'd have my St Egbert's Irregulars. The Baker Street version was a bunch of kids who went out scouting around on Holmes's behalf, forming a secret network of eyes that could keep watch on suspicious persons.

So the following break-time, I enlisted the help of a gang of eager tinies from the Reception class. Follow Thug Robinson, I told them, watch his every move, you are my secret network of eyes.

Twenty-four hours later, they reported back. Three of them had taken me literally, and had to be collected by angry parents from off Thug's doorstep. Five had got the wrong Robinson, and told me all about Sally Robinson's dolly that said 'mama'. The rest of them turned up and said they'd seen Thug captured by aliens from a pirate ship, definitely, true, honest, and could they have the pound coins I'd promised them now?

So much for that. If you want a job doing properly, do it yourself!

I collected Watson and off we went. Thug wasn't a difficult person to trail. If you lost sight of his chunky frame in the crowd, you could always follow the sound of arms being twisted.

We managed to keep track of his movements for over half the following week, without getting a single significant clue. Everywhere he went, people got out of his way if they saw him coming or, if they didn't see him coming, soon wished they could get out of his way.

Until!

It was nearly going-home time, Wednesday. They were repainting the school gates (following an unfortunate incident with a bag of jam doughnuts and Sickly O'Sullivan's stomach), so we all had to leave via the side exit that the older kids from the senior school usually used.

I grabbed Watson by the collar and dragged him into the shadows by the Modern Languages block.

'What?' he demanded, spraying a mouthful of crumbs everywhere. 'I nearly dropped me pasty.'

'Look!' I said, putting on the intense, hawk-like expression that had taken me hours to perfect in the bathroom mirror. 'Look who Thug's with!'

Thug was talking to a very smart boy with very neat hair and very small glasses. The boy was chatting amiably, and so was Thug.

'Who's that then?' said Watson.

'I have absolutely no idea,' I said. I was pretty sure I'd seen him in school assemblies being presented with prizes. 'I think he's in the year above us. Or possibly the year above that.'

'And why does it matter?' said Watson.

'Oh, for goodness' sake, Watson,' I sighed. 'Look at them! Thug's being friendly! He doesn't do that any other time, does he? That kid could be significant!'

I waited for Thug to be on his way. Then, as the boy approached, I sprang from the shadows, pulling Watson after me. Sherlock Holmes was a master of disguise, possessing an uncanny ability which aided him many times in his quest for the truth.

I put on a thick Scottish accent. 'Och aye, hallo!'

The boy stopped, and blinked at me nervously. 'Hallo?' he said. 'Do I know you? Sorry, chaps, must dash, I'm late for choir practice.' He had a very posh voice, too. I had an inkling as to who he was now. I just couldn't recall his name.

'Aye, laddy,' I said, 'just a wee word. Ma friend here and I were jus' thinking, was that Thug Robinson you were talkin' to back there? Only I said that a lad like yourself, errr . . . Angus, a lad like yourself wouldnae be—'

'My name's not Angus,' said the boy, 'it's Maurice.'

Of course! Mega-Maurice! The brainiest pupil in the school! The kid was a legend. He was the one who'd rewired all the computers in the IT Room, after they'd been cleaned of a virus the year before.

'So, umm, how do you know Thug Robinson, hoots mon?' I said.

'He's our cleaning lady at home,' said Maurice.

Watson's eyes widened. Mine narrowed.

'Well, not "lady", of course,' said Maurice. 'But he pops in and tidies up every day after school. He's pretty good at it, and charges a very reasonable rate. He does my room a treat. I wouldn't have thought him capable, personally, but it just goes to show there's good in everyone.'

'And, err, he simply volunteered for this, did he?' I said.

'Yes,' said Maurice. 'He lives next door to us. I had to baby-sit the nasty little worm during half term. He wouldn't stop tampering with my PC. But you can't print or e-mail without a password, so he didn't do any damage, fortunately. Anyway, I happened to mention that our last cleaning lady had run off to join the circus and all of a sudden he was nice as pie and said he'd do it. I'd thought he was a right horror at first, but I've got to admit I was wrong.'

'Och, aye,' I said, 'he's a great wee laddy.'

'Look,' said Maurice crossly, 'why are you so interested in who cleans my room? Are you after something? And what's with the stupid fake accent? Eh?'

We were faced with extremely awkward questions, so Watson and I did what any crime-fighting duo in our position would have done. We ran away.

Apart from a stop-over for Watson to get a hamburger, it was full speed back to my house all the way. I was feeling rather chuffed.

'I'm feeling rather confused,' said Watson, stuffing down the last of his sesame bun.

'On the contrary, Watson,' I said confidently. 'Things become clearer every minute.'

'Clearer how exactly?' said Watson, after a tum-loosening belch.

'All we have to do now is infiltrate Thug Robinson's room.'

I won't go into Watson's reaction. Let's just say it wasn't polite. But it was vital to get a look at Thug's room, to confirm my suspicions. Or at least, to give me a few final clues to the whole story.

'If I'm right,' I said, 'we'll find an old and clunky computer in there.'

Getting into Thug's house proved easier than I'd imagined. We waited until we knew Thug was out frightening toddlers in the park, and swooped. I rang the doorbell.

Thug's dad appeared, scratching his bum. He had a big, grubby plaster stuck to his forehead. He was completely fooled by our blue overalls, fake ID cards, and false moustaches.

'Is everyone from the electric company as short as you two?' he said, scratching his leg.

'Oh, yes, sir,' I said. 'Requirement of the job. In case we need to squeeze into any confined spaces. Now, we've had reports of dangerous wiring in this street, so we're having to check every premises, especially the upstairs.'

'Be my guest,' said Thug's dad, scratching his head. 'But I'm not doin' you a cup of tea.'

Thug's room was disgusting. No, worse than

disgusting. We didn't dare touch anything for fear of contracting a disease.

But!

The vital clue was there, just as I'd expected. Sitting on a chipped sideboard that was overflowing with stained T-shirts. The PC was not only old and clunky, it was—and this was the decider—dented on top. There was a sharp V-shape in its CPU case, which had split the machine's CD-ROM tray, making it unusable.

I switched the computer on and it wheezed into life. From the pocket of my overalls I produced a floppy disk, and copied its contents on to the hard drive.

'What are you *doing*?' hissed Watson.

'On this disk is the virus they cleaned off the computers in the IT Room last year. Sherlock Holmes collected odd bits of kit, and so do I. It scrambles files so they look OK but read like gobbledegook.'

Watson hissed a few more questions at me, but when did you ever hear of a detective revealing the plot before the final scene? Quite.

We reassured Thug's dad that his wiring was absolutely fine, and made a hasty retreat. Just in time too—Thug was coming down the street as we dashed off in the opposite direction.

Right. Final scene.

Class, the next morning. We all hand in our homework on the life of Charles Dickens. Thug gives his to Mrs Womsey with his now-usual smug grin. She flicks through it.

'Jonathan,' she said quietly. 'This is nonsense. This is gobbledegook. Dickens was not a puff adder. Neither was he French, nor the inventor of the nuclear explosion. You've been doing so well lately, and now you've gone back to your old ways.'

Thug looked shocked. Watson looked amazed. I looked pretty darn cool.

Of course, after that, Thug's brief reign as class brainbox was over. His homework plummeted back into the gutter from whence it came, and good riddance.

'How?' said Watson, admiringly. 'Why, when, where, and what?'

'Elementary,' I said calmly. 'Thug sees Mega-Maurice's room in half term. More specifically, his PC, packed with all the brilliant, teacher-pleasing homework he's ever done. Maurice is a year or two ahead of us, therefore he's already done all the homework that we're being set now. Thug spots an opportunity to cheat. But, oh dear, he's a right thicko and parts of Maurice's PC are passworded. He can't print or e-mail Maurice's old homework. He can download it, though; even he can manage that. But, oh dear again, his own PC is dented. His CD-ROM is broken. He can't copy lots of files. All he can copy is one floppy disk's worth at a time. And if he's going to do that, he needs regular access to Maurice's computer. So he volunteers to be a cleaning lady, and every day, while Maurice isn't looking, he copies another disk's-worth of info, whatever is that night's homework. He takes it home, prints it out, or copies it down in his own scrawly handwriting, and bingo. He's top of the class.'

'And the virus means that every file he tries to copy now will come out scrambled,' said Watson.

I sat back and gazed out of the window. To have a mind as brilliant as mine is a gift, and I intend to share that gift with the world. I'm thinking of taking up the violin.

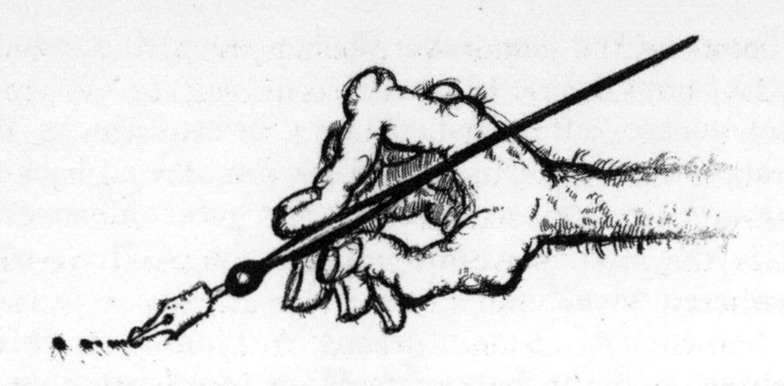

Rodier's Necklace

LINDA NEWBERY

It was the eve of the wedding, and every maid and man, every cook and groom and kitchen boy, was busy with preparations. The daughter of the house, Rosamond, was to be married next day to Lord Geraint. Already she had more gifts than she could count: a whole room had been set aside for them. There was gold, silver, precious jewels, fine cloths; there were goblets on the table and rose-bowls on the chairs, shrouded items piled on the floor and smaller ones on the mantel; a kingfisher-coloured bird piped from a cage wrought of silver. Rosamond glanced in at the enticing heaps, but had no time now to examine them more closely. Her maidservant was preparing a scented bath in her chamber, and she intended to be early abed on this last night before her new life began.

It was to be a Yuletide wedding. Fires burned in every grate, and the fireplaces and sconces were decorated with holly and with ivy, with pine cones and yew and bunches of mistletoe. Tomorrow, after the wedding ceremony, there would be a great feast, and all the rooms of the manor were being prepared for guests. All day, housemaids had been scrubbing and sweeping, footmen cleaning the pewter and the silverware, boys heaping fresh-sawn logs beside every fireplace, cooks roasting and basting in the kitchen. Out in the stables the grooms were tending the horses, especially Snowberry, Rosamond's own white mare, and polishing the harness. Rosamond drifted from room to room, touching a holly spray here, a candlestick there, nibbling a crystallized grape, taking a stem of winter jasmine from a vase. All this for me! she thought. For me and for Geraint. And she thought with satisfaction of her choice; for she had been courted by many a young nobleman and had taken her time before settling on handsome, dark-haired Geraint, who looked so splendid on his black horse, and rode so fearlessly. Geraint and I, she thought, will be a perfectly-matched bride and groom. Everyone will say so. And she looked at her reflection in the mirror, at the perfect oval of her face surrounded by braided hair as black and glossy as a raven's wing, and she was pleased with what she saw.

Outside at the gatehouse, where twilight deepened the shade beneath the oaks and an owl drifted like a great white moth, the gatekeeper was awoken from his doze by hoofbeats on the leaf track. Guiltily, he pulled himself to attention. The rider slowed his horse, a magnificent bay, and made it stand.

'I bring a gift for Lady Rosamond,' said the stranger. 'I must give it to her myself.'

'What, at this hour?' The gatekeeper stretched stiff arms and legs. 'Hand it to me, sirrah, and I'll see she gets it.'

He stretched up a hand, looking at the stranger's face. Even in the fading light he could see that the horseman was a handsome young man, well-built and strong. His eyes were dark and brown. One hand held the reins, the other a small parcel. His bay horse looked mettlesome, but he sat it easily.

'Here,' said the gatekeeper with a touch of impatience, still reaching up for the parcel.

The rider shook his head. 'I must give it to the lady myself.'

'Oh, very well,' said the gatekeeper; the newcomer had the look of a man who would not be gainsaid. 'Follow me. I'll see if my lady's maidservant can come down to you.'

The bay horse, he noticed, looked uneasy as it entered the courtyard; it pranced and side-stepped. Its rider soothed and calmed it, stroking its mane with a gentle hand.

'Who shall I say is here?' asked the gatekeeper, curious.

'My name is Rodier,' said the horseman.

Alice, the maidservant, came down to the courtyard, but this was not good enough for the visitor. 'I must speak to your mistress in person,' he insisted. 'Please ask her to come down.'

'Well—' Alice was doubtful. 'It's late, but—I'll ask.'

Up in the bedchamber, Rosamond was preparing to take her bath and was impatient at her maid's absence; but the news intrigued her. 'There's a very handsome brown-eyed man wants to speak to you in the courtyard, my lady,' said Alice. 'Rodier, he said his name is.'

'Rodier? Lord Rodier? Earl or Duke, perhaps? Of noble blood, surely? No commoner would have the impertinence to come to my door and demand an audience!'

'I'm afraid he didn't say, my lady. Just Rodier.'

'A French nobleman, maybe? And—handsome, you said?'

'*Very* handsome, my lady. Should I fetch your father? Have him sent away?'

'No—no. I will go down and see for myself.' Rosamond put on a warm wrap and slipped on her shoes. Keeping a careful look-out for her father, she went down to the entrance hall and out to the steps. She shivered in the cold evening air, and pulled her wrap more tightly around her.

'Yes?' she called. 'Who is it demands to see me?'

The gatekeeper, banging his arms against his sides to keep warm, watched as the stranger rode his horse right up to the open door, leaned down from his saddle and handed Rosamond the small package he carried. Then he bent down to speak to her. Strain his ears as he might, the gatekeeper could not make out the words that were exchanged.

A disappointed suitor, that's my guess, he thought.

The conversation did not last more than a few moments. The visitor straightened in his saddle, turned his horse and clopped out of the courtyard, raising a hand in thanks to the gatekeeper. In the light of the torch-flames his hair looked for a moment the colour of autumn beech leaves.

Slowly, Rosamond climbed the stairs to her bedchamber. The stranger's gift was wrapped in some gauzy material that looked like the skeletons of last year's leaves. She paused outside her room to pull the leafy stuff aside and reveal the heavier object it concealed. It was a necklace—a strand of diamonds and rubies that caught the glow of candlelight and winked and darted it back at her.

'Oh, how beautiful—perfect!' she whispered. And she thought of the stranger's dark, dark eyes, and how they had seemed to pierce her to the soul. She went into her chamber to show Alice the gift.

Rodier's words she would keep to herself.

'I implore you,' he had said, in a deep low voice she longed to hear more of, 'do not go hunting on St Stephen's Day. Promise me you will not.'

It was an outrageous request! Everything was arranged—the horses groomed, the hounds kept hungry, the guests invited. There could be no question of abandoning the hunting party at the whim of an unknown admirer, no matter how handsome he might be, how large and full his eyes or how deep and persuasive his gaze. It was impossible to agree to his request. She knew this even while she gazed back at him and said:

'Yes. Yes, I promise.'

Christmas Day arrived, the day of the wedding, and guests arrived from near and far. In her dress of cobweb-grey, with her hair braided and coiled and netted with fine-spun silk, Rosamond knew that she looked more beautiful than ever before. After the marriage ceremony in the chapel, the bride and groom and their guests took their seats in the Great Hall. The tables were decked with winter flowers, with bowls piled high with fruit, with pastries and sweetmeats. Candle-flames lit the faces of the hundred guests and sparkled on the crystal and silver. But the eyes of everyone present were drawn to Lady Rosamond where she sat beside her new husband. Around her neck glowed the rubies and diamonds of Rodier's necklace.

'That is a beautiful necklace,' Geraint said to his bride; 'perfect, against the silver-grey of your dress. I have never seen you wear it before.'

Rosamond touched the jewels, and thought of the mysterious giver. 'It was a gift from a stranger.'

Geraint frowned, because he had given her many jewels. 'If you prefer a stranger's gift to mine, I will give you another necklace, one with richer jewels still.'

'But this one is all I could want,' Rosamond said. Then she held out her left hand and spread her fingers so that the beaten gold ring she wore, engraved with an intricate design, caught the light from the candles. 'I am wearing your ring today, and surely that makes you happy!'

And she smiled secretively as she thought of her unknown suitor, and Geraint said no more, for he would not quarrel with his bride on their wedding day. But he vowed that he would take the diamond and ruby necklace from her.

St Stephen's Day dawned cold, bright with winter sunshine. It was a crisp scenting day, perfect for the hunting party, and soon the hounds were giving voice and setting off at a brisk pace into the depths of the forest. Rosamond and her husband rode side by side, she on Snowberry, he on a tall black horse whose tail was so long that it swept the ground. The guests marvelled at the picture they made, beautiful Rosamond on her white mare, and the handsome young nobleman by her side. But Geraint was sore at heart, because his bride had once again put on the ruby and diamond necklace. He had asked her instead to wear a strand of sea-pearls which he had given her on their betrothal, but she said, 'The rubies are a better match for my scarlet riding-habit.' And now as he looked he saw that the rubies and diamonds were indeed perfect against her clear skin, and her raven's-wing hair.

Rosamond too was ill at ease, remembering her promise—the promise she had never intended to keep. But who was Rodier? she thought, smoothing Snowberry's mane. I shall never see him again. A pity—how I long to look deep into those eyes again, and be held by their spell! And she told herself, with guilty pleasure, that a newly-married lady should not have such secrets.

Rosamond, though a lady, was known as a fearless rider to hounds. And Snowberry, though she was gentle and milk-white, was fleet of foot and nimbler than the bigger horses. The other members of the hunting party were used to seeing only Snowberry's plumy tail, as Rosamond urged her faster beneath the great trees.

Today the hound-pack found a splendid buck, a roe, with branched antlers—a fit quarry for the wedding party. The hounds gave tongue, and ran on like a tumbling stream. Horses and riders followed through thickets and clearings, deep, deep into the quiet heart of the forest, where the river carved its path between mossy banks. At last the deer, which had outpaced the hounds at first with agile leaps, was exhausted, and could run no more. He stood at bay beneath an ancient oak to face the hounds as they encircled him. Rosamond pushed through the thicket of holly and thorn beside the huntsman, Geraint close behind her, and looked at the brave, beaten animal.

'He has given us good sport, and now he will give us good venison,' she said.

The huntsman dismounted, pulled his knife from his belt, and waded through the leaping hounds. Rosamond watched, and saw shining silver tears drop from the deer's eyes and fall into the waters of the stream. Instead of melting into the flow, the tears sank like stones to lie on the sandy bed of the river, glinting and sparkling. And now the doomed buck was staring directly at her, his eyes fixed on hers, almost as if he would speak. His eyes were large, and dark, darkest brown.

My promise! she thought.

The huntsman's blade flashed at the buck's throat. As the blood flowed, and the magnificent beast sagged to the ground, Rosamond saw that a small stream of scarlet reached the river and separated into drops, like deep glowing rubies, which sank into the waters and settled on the sandy bed. The deer was a lifeless weight, his proud, antlered head lolling against the moss of the river bank.

'What is it?' asked Geraint, seeing his bride's distress. 'What ails you, beloved?'

'My promise,' Rosamond whispered again, unable to forget that last look. Her sides heaved. She felt her eyes widening with terror. She panted for breath, as if she had run for her life, and spent her last gasp. She clutched at her throat.

Geraint saw the ruby and silver necklace flashing its points of light, and he took his chance. He snatched at the necklace, snapping the silver clasp; then he hurled it with all his strength and watched it rise in a shimmering arc to drop into the stream without a splash, and sink from view. And Rosamond gazed without speaking at the place where it had fallen, and she began to breathe again.

When the deer had been gutted and the tripes thrown to the hounds, it was lashed by its hooves to strong poles so that it could be carried back to the manor. Soon nothing was left of the hunt but the hoofmarks on the river bank and a dark stain on the mossy ground.

All the animals of the forest, scenting fear and death, avoided the place for a long time to come.

Rosamond had lost the taste for venison. She rode back to the manor, downcast, and would not speak to anyone, not even her new husband. She grieved alone in her room. Next day she sent one of the grooms to retrieve her necklace from the stream, but although the man waded back and forth till he was numb with cold, the necklace was never seen again. To make up for its loss, Geraint gave his bride necklaces of pearl, of emerald and of sapphire, but never of ruby or diamond.

After the wedding festivities were over, Rosamond went to live with Geraint in another part of the forest. Whenever hunting parties set out on a crisp winter's day, she remained at home, and Snowberry stayed in her stable. Rosamond watched from her casement as the horses and hounds made their way into the forest. And when her sides heaved for breath and her eyes filled with tears for the exhausted buck, she knew that the huntsman was about to make a kill.

A year turned, and another winter stripped the forest bare. On Yuletide Eve, Rosamond sat nursing her baby daughter, Fawna. Geraint was late to bed, having made sure all preparations had been made for the morrow's hunting party: the horses groomed, the hounds hungry, the harness polished and shining. Rosamond was sad, as she always was on the eve of a hunting day. She had never been able to make her husband understand why she had lost all pleasure in the chase. Many a time she had implored him not to hunt, but he swept aside her pleas, and mocked her: 'What woman's foolishness is this?' So she kept her thoughts to herself, but nothing he said could tempt her to ride to hounds, even though it had given her such delight. She had broken her promise once; she would not break it again. And whenever she looked at her baby daughter, she was reminded of the stranger's dark, dark eyes; for Fawna had eyes as soft and brown as a deer's.

She was tucking the baby girl into her cradle when her husband's manservant knocked on the door of the chamber.

'My lord, there is a young woman at the door who insists on speaking to you. She says she has some gift which she must give to you herself.'

Rosamond caught her breath.

'Her name?' said Geraint.

'Rodier, my lord. I believe that's what she said. Whether it was Lady Rodier or Countess Rodier she did not say.'

'French, perhaps?' said Geraint, caught with curiosity. 'What manner of young woman is she?'

The manservant smiled. 'Hard to say, my lord. But she's well-favoured—very well-favoured indeed.'

'Maybe I should go and see for myself,' said Geraint. He glanced at Rosamond, who knew well enough how he could be beguiled by shining eyes and gentle looks. She was tempted to go herself to the courtyard, to see if the young woman had the same deep, penetrating eyes as her masculine counterpart; the reproachful eyes that gazed at her in dreams and pierced her heart.

But the message this time was for Geraint.

'Go, my love,' she urged him. 'Go, and accept what she has to give you.'

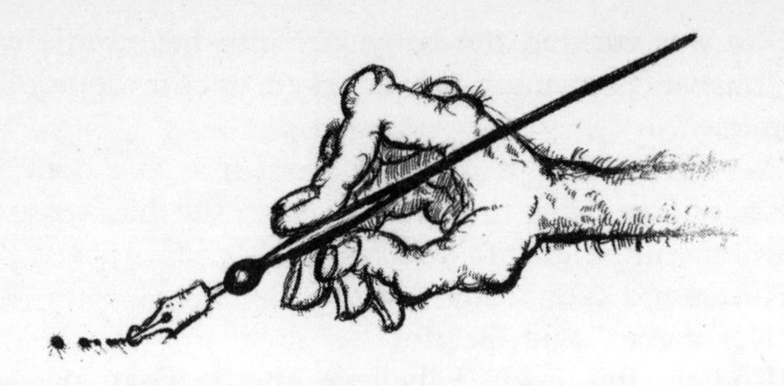

Bad Presents

DAVID BELBIN

They took it in turn to open presents in front of the fire. Brett unwrapped a video-shaped one 'from Auntie Pat'. It turned out to be a book. Brett hated books.

'Rubbish!' he said, throwing it into the fire.

Craig chose next. 'Feels like a DVD,' he said. But it was only a double CD of classical music. He cursed and aimed it at the fire.

'Hold on!' Brett said. 'You might be able to sell that.'

Craig put it aside.

'Let's try the big ones,' Brett suggested. He opened a heavy box. He was hoping it would be a Playstation 2, but it turned out to be an expensive hairdryer.

'Give it here,' Craig said. 'My mum can have that for Christmas.'

'And how will she think you afforded it?'

'Mum knows better than to ask questions like that,' Craig said. 'Next?'

'I need a drink,' Brett said, pulling out a brightly wrapped bottle. 'This came from the big house on the hill. Should be something good.'

The big house had been their final burglary of the night. Craig hoped for vodka. Brett would have settled for wine. But it was some green muck.

'Let's pour it on the fire,' Craig said.

'No, wait,' Brett told him. 'I've heard of this Absinthe stuff! It's meant to blow your head off.'

'Go on, then,' Craig told him. 'Let's open it.'

Brett pulled out the cork and took a swig from the bottle.

'That's horrible,' he said, handing the drink to Craig, who took a swig.

'Goes straight to your head, though,' Craig said. 'Let's try those kids' presents. I need something for my little sister. She's into Walt Disney. And dolls. Any of them look like a Barbie?'

They set about opening the rest of the stolen presents.

Christmas at the Coopers was miserable this year. Only the family were there. The housekeeper, Mrs Phelps, had been given Christmas off to visit her daughter in Oban. Martin, Mr Cooper's eldest son, was newly divorced and back living at home. At nine, he was still sleeping off the two bottles of wine he'd downed on Christmas Eve. His brother Gordon was still in bed. He was thinking about his mother, who had died in a car crash six months before. This Christmas, the huge house sorely lacked a woman's touch. Gordon was in no rush to go downstairs and open his presents.

The house had thick walls, but the windows were old and single glazed. On stormy nights, the weather kept Gordon awake. They lived on the top of a hill, so he was rarely bothered by the sound of traffic. At five past nine, however, he heard a police siren. It sounded as if it was coming from downhill. Gordon wondered what had happened to bring the police out on a day like today.

The siren grew louder and louder, as though the car were climbing the hill. There were only three other houses on this road. Which neighbours had called the police? The mayor and her husband? The retired hospital consultant? Or the Euro MP? Outside, the siren abruptly stopped. Gordon got out of bed and opened the curtains, letting in a chilly Scottish draught. A police car was parked in the drive. Dad, still in his dressing gown, was out there to meet it.

'You don't have a burglar alarm?' the officer asked Gordon's father.

'We do, but we only turn it on when we go away,' Mr Cooper explained. 'With two boys in the house, they'd be setting it off all hours.'

'Two boys you say. This one would be . . . ' He pointed at the scrawny youth on the stairs, who was wearing tracksuit bottoms and an Arran sweater.

'This is Gordon. My other son is Martin. I still think of him as a boy, though he's in his twenties. He's living here at the moment.'

'Could you tell me—approximately—how many presents were taken?'

Only now did Gordon look under the tree, where only a handful of presents remained. Although wrapped, their contents were obvious. The burglars had left behind the books. Gordon and his father read a lot.

'About half a dozen,' Mr Cooper said.

'Are you sure that's all?'

'It's a small family,' Mr Cooper explained. 'Most of the presents were for my younger son, Gordon. Martin and I aren't too bothered.'

Martin appeared at the top of the stairs, still in his boxer shorts.

'If you wouldn't mind joining us, sir,' the officer said. 'I'm going to need a list of all the presents stolen.'

'That's easier said than done,' Mr Cooper said. 'The three of us know what we were giving each other, but as for other people, I don't see how . . . '

'You could ring them,' the officer suggested. 'There weren't very many, after all.'

'I don't understand the point,' Mr Cooper said. 'I'm hardly going to bother claiming on the insurance for a handful of presents.'

'You might not need to,' the police officer told him. 'Earlier this morning, we recovered some stolen Christmas presents. It's possible yours were among them. We'd like you to come to the station in an hour or so to identify what belongs to you. But if you don't know what the presents were, that may be a little difficult.'

An hour later, the Coopers drove to the police station. Gordon had phoned round relatives while his dad put the turkey on. He knew what was inside most of the missing packages. The three had eaten a quick breakfast and exchanged what presents the burglars had left behind.

'I bought you a bottle as well, Dad,' Martin said in the car. 'A good one.'

'Let's hope the burglars didn't drink it.'

'What did you get me?' Gordon asked, as they pulled up at the station.

'I'll tell you when we see it,' Martin replied.

There was another family leaving the police station as the Coopers arrived. The woman was holding an expensive hairdryer.

'Never thought I'd see that again,' her husband said, chuckling to himself.

'Wonder how they caught them,' the son asked, clutching three computer games. They ignored the Coopers as they walked past them. Gordon looked enviously at the computer games.

They were greeted by a young CID officer, Detective Constable Clarke. No senior officer would work on Christmas day, Mr Cooper guessed.

'I won't take too much of your time,' DC Clarke said. 'As far as we can tell, the burglars raided three houses, of which yours was the last. One family's already identified their property and the other family will be along shortly.'

'How did you catch the thieves?' Martin asked.

'We didn't,' the DC replied. 'In a sense, they gave themselves up. Now, before we start, you say there were six presents missing . . . '

'Six or seven,' Mr Cooper said. 'We couldn't quite agree on the number.'

'Why would that be?'

'Mrs Phelps, our housekeeper, may have left us something under the tree.'

'And where is she?'

'At her daughter's,' Mr Cooper replied.

'Do you have a phone number for her?'

'Yes, but I don't see why . . . '

'We like to be very thorough,' DC Clarke interrupted, then wrote the number down. 'Let's take a look, shall we? Follow me.'

The unwrapped presents were on a trestle table in the police canteen. Mr Cooper recognized the Playstation game he'd bought for Martin. Gordon pointed out the double classical CD he'd got for his dad.

'Very nice,' Mr Cooper said to him. 'Now, where's yours? I say, somebody has been at this bottle.'

'I'm afraid so,' the DC said. 'They'd drunk half of it before we caught them. Absinthe. The proper stuff, not the rubbish you get in the shops here. People buy it on the Internet and have it sent over from France or Holland. Is it yours?'

'I don't know.' Mr Cooper turned to Martin. 'Didn't you say you'd got me a bottle?'

'Don't think you'd like that poison,' Martin said. 'It's more my style. No, I got you that bottle of Glendronach on the end there.'

'How about you, Gordon,' the CID man said. 'Did you buy the bottle?'

'I'm too young to buy alcohol,' Gordon said. 'It must belong to the other family, the ones who haven't had a look yet.'

'I don't think so,' the CID man said. 'They're teetotallers.'

Gordon looked at the remaining presents: a sweater, some perfume, two boxes of chocolates, three fluffy animals, and a big, boring board game. They didn't look as if they belonged to the sort of people who drank Absinthe.

A police officer came in and whispered something to DC Clarke.

'Mrs Phelps confirms that she didn't buy the bottle,' he told the Coopers. 'But she says that there were definitely two bottles under the tree when she left yesterday morning. So the question remains, which of you bought the Absinthe?'

'I really don't understand why this is so important,' Mr Cooper said. 'After all, even if it belongs to one of us, we're not going to drink the stuff when we don't know what low life has been glugging away at it.'

'Quite so,' the DC said. 'But perhaps we can go over who gave what to whom one more time? What did you get for Gordon, Mr Cooper?'

'A computer game. Which seems to be missing, by the way.'

'Was it the latest *Civilization*?' Gordon asked, angrily.

'That's right.'

'The lad who was here before pretended it was his.'

The CID man made a note, then made a rather personal comment. 'I believe that Martin and Gordon have different mothers.'

'Yes,' Mr Cooper said. 'Martin's mother died soon after our marriage. We lost Gordon's mother in a car crash last June.'

'And when you die, sir, do both of your sons get an equal share of your wealth?'

'What kind of question is that?' Mr Cooper snapped.

'An important one,' the DC said in a calming voice. 'I believe that your first wife came from a large brewing family.'

'Yes, that's where the money comes from. And, yes, Martin gets most of it. Gordon would be decently provided for, of course. But I don't see what business it is of yours.'

'The thing is,' DC Clarke gave each one in turn a long hard stare. 'One of you is lying. I'm going to keep you here until I find out which of you it is.'

'That's outrageous!' Mr Cooper said. 'I want my solicitor!'

The CID man suddenly seemed older, more confident. 'You might have trouble finding him on Christmas day,' he said.

'It's a her. And we're leaving. You've no right to keep us here unless you arrest us!'

'Very well, then,' they were told. 'You're all under arrest.'

'On what charge?' Martin demanded.

The officer spoke softly and without emotion. 'The manslaughter of Craig Fettes and Brett Macdonald early this morning.'

Mrs Luithlen, the family solicitor, arrived just as the Coopers should have been tucking into their Christmas dinner.

'This is all some kind of misunderstanding, I'm sure,' she said. 'Trouble is, I can't contact the Inspector in charge, only the young man who dealt with you. And he's playing his cards very close to his chest.'

'What happened?' Martin wanted to know.

'It's very simple,' Mrs Luithlen said. 'The two young men who broke into your house drank half a bottle of Absinthe when they got back to their squat. It was poisoned. One of them managed to call an ambulance on his mobile before he passed out. But they were both dead before the emergency services got there.'

'Why do they assume that the Absinthe came from us?' Mr Cooper asked. 'I mean, these people probably bought the drink themselves on the black market.'

'Absinthe's not very popular on council estates,' Mrs Luithlen said. 'It's more of a trendy drink for the well off. And the taste is so strong that it disguises almost any poison. The rest of the bottle is being tested now, then we'll know what the poison was. My question is, who would want to kill one or all of you?'

'The bottle couldn't have been meant for Gordon,' Martin pointed out. 'He's too young to drink.'

'Is there anybody with a grudge against you?' the solicitor asked Martin.

'Only my ex-wife. But she left me. We made a fair divorce settlement. Is there any water to drink in here? I'm really dehydrated.'

Before Mrs Luithlen could answer, the door opened. It was DC Clarke, accompanied by a middle-aged Detective Inspector.

'Which of you is Martin Cooper?' the DI asked.

Martin stepped forward. 'I am.'

'I'm charging you with the attempted murder of your father and the manslaughter of Craig Fettes and Brett Macdonald.'

Martin looked flabbergasted. 'But that's ridiculous. What proof do you have? I didn't buy the Absinthe!'

'That's right,' Gordon argued. 'Martin bought Dad a bottle of malt whisky. You might as well blame me. After all, you haven't found the present that I bought for Martin. I might have bought the poisoned bottle for him.'

'But you didn't,' the Detective Inspector said. 'You see, we found a second bottle of Absinthe hidden in Martin's room. He'd meant to switch the bottles after his father had drunk the one laced with cyanide.'

'This is preposterous,' Mr Cooper said. 'What motive does Martin have for killing me? After all, he already inherits most of the family money when I die.'

'Your son has no job and still lives at home,' the DI pointed out. 'Maybe he'd like his money now.'

They handcuffed Martin. 'I'm sure we'll get you out soon,' Mrs Luithlen told him. 'The evidence against you is purely circumstantial.'

Mr Cooper and his youngest son drove home alone.

'I can't believe that Martin would act that way,' Mr

Cooper said. 'He's selfish and lazy, I admit, but to think he'd murder me! It must be a mistake.'

'He has been acting pretty strangely this year,' Gordon said. 'Not that I'm suggesting he did it. Only, maybe if the balance of his mind was disturbed . . . '

'We have to believe him,' Mr Cooper insisted, 'unless more evidence against him appears. Otherwise, old son, it's just you and me.'

More evidence would appear, Gordon knew that. He had ordered the two bottles of Absinthe on the Internet, using Martin's computer and credit card number. It wouldn't take CID long to find that out. It was lucky that Gordon had thought to hide the second bottle in Martin's room. He'd meant to switch the bottles and make it look like suicide.

In some ways, the way things had worked out was better than his original plan. There'd always been a risk that Dad would get hurt (the Absinthe was intended for Martin, not his father, but both men liked a drink). As it was, Martin was bound to be disinherited. Everything would come to Gordon. Which would serve Martin right. He'd been driving the car which crashed last spring. Martin, drunk, and not wearing a seat belt, had been thrown clear in the collision. Gordon's mum was not so lucky.

Father and son got home to the smell of burning turkey.

'Can't say I'm hungry anyhow,' Mr Cooper muttered.

'I wonder what happened to the DVD I bought for Martin,' Gordon said.

'Maybe the burglars dropped it,' Mr Cooper suggested. 'Or the other family took that, too.'

'You're right,' said Gordon. 'You can't trust anyone these days.'

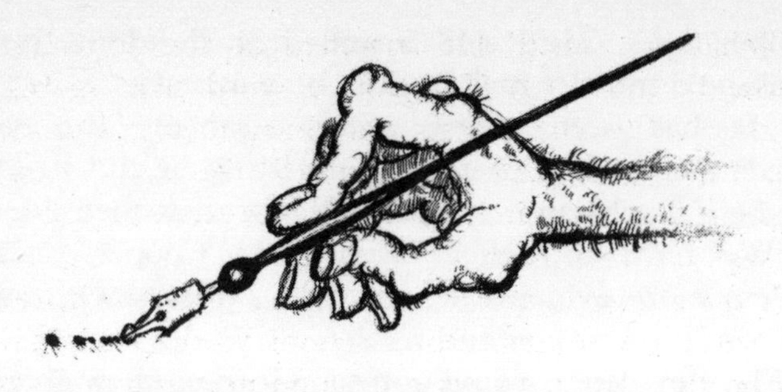

Gone Away

JOHN GORDON

Is there anyone there?
Listen! Don't go away!
Answer me. Please!

The school was dark. In the noiseless corridors the shadows leant against the walls like weary sentries and nothing stirred. And then, somewhere unseen, a door opened and closed and footsteps approached the long row of empty classrooms.

The cleaners had long since gone home and left Bob Harte to lock up. It had been a long day. There had been a staff meeting after school, then a stack of papers to work through, and rather than cart it all home he had stayed on to finish it, so that now he was weary and not at all in a good temper. He was yawning and, to tell the truth, he had closed his eyes for a few steps so he did not see the computer screen suddenly wake up. The classroom was almost behind him when, from the corner of his eye, he saw the glow through the glass of the door.

'What the devil!' He snatched at the door handle. 'Those little . . . !' He spoke a word that no teacher should use of his pupils and barged into the room. 'Don't they ever turn anything off?' But even as he was reaching for the switch his tired eyes were taking in the message on the screen.

Is there anyone there? . . . but he read no further. It was some bit of unfinished school work. His fingertip was on the button to erase it when new words flickered into life at the foot of the screen: *wait wait wait!!!*

No capital letters, he noticed—Bob Harte was an English teacher. He thought he must have accidentally touched the scroll button but the message ended there. He went to the top of the page and read it all, down to *Answer me. Please!* It was a meaningless paragraph. He sighed, closed his eyes, and yawned. When he opened them the screen was blank . . . except that new words were unrolling: *mr harte its about me it is it is!!!*

No punctuation worth thinking of, but a clever stunt nevertheless. Some young dog of a trickster had him under observation from somewhere outside and was tapping away on a laptop. He pushed back his chair and was about to step to the window to look out when it happened again.

Dont go Mr Harte dont go!

In spite of himself, Bob was amused. He sat at the keyboard and typed: 'You're improving, but you should put an apostrophe in don't.'

Don't worry, Mr Harte, I'll get it right if you stay to listen.

Cheeky young devil, but he hardly bothered to read. He was searching the screen. If he was exchanging messages with some trickster that must mean the computer was on the Internet. But this was no e-mail, simply a plain screen.

He went back to the keyboard. 'How are you doing this?' But his question was ignored and the next message made his face harden with anger.

I am someone you know. I am Sophie.

He banged at the keys: 'Stop! I will have no more of this!' He pushed his chair away from the screen. Whoever was watching would see that the joke was over.

Stay!

No, he would not stay. He would not tolerate any jokes about what had happened to Sophie Wade. He stood up.

please mr harte dont leave me please please

No capitals, no commas, no exclamation marks . . . his teacher's eye noticed this but at the same time he sensed the panic in the words. He hesitated.

I have to talk to you, Mr Harte. Will you please sit down?

That seemed calmer. He fought down the urge to turn his back. Everyone knew that Sophie Wade had been missing for ten days. What this cruel hoaxer obviously did not know was that it was impossible for her to be speaking to him or to anyone else. Sophie, the youngest girl in his class, had been found late that very afternoon and was now lying in hospital, unconscious. He knew he must track down the savage mind that mocked a dying girl. His fingers spelled out, 'Tell me how you can see me.'

I can only see you when you are close to the screen.

That made some sort of sense, but it was not nearly enough. He asked, 'Where are you?' There was a pause before the screen came to life.

I don't really know.

That was no answer. The hoaxer was wasting time. 'Tell me, or I leave.'

Again a pause but then, suddenly, a rush of words.

It is always dark in here and it makes me sleep. Sometimes I hear machinery. It just buzzes very quietly but I cannot seem to touch it. Not long ago I thought someone came in and I ran towards the place but I fell over and everything went black. When I woke up I saw this screen. It is very dim but I see the classroom through it.

The hoaxer also had a keyboard and seemed to be telling him that his own screen was some sort of window. He leant close to it but not even his own face was reflected in the glass. 'Try harder. I don't believe you.'

There must be a video camera somewhere. He stretched and turned, looking around the room. There was nothing. Words began to appear on the screen but anger made him ignore them and he discovered he could type over them and blot them out. 'Listen to me . . . If you tell me who you are, truthfully, this will go no further. I can take a joke. But if you insist on pretending to be that poor girl, I will seek you out and you will be in real trouble. Do you understand?' It was like shouting down a noisy class. The screen went dumb.

And then, like a small, quiet voice, as if it was afraid to speak at all, timid words crept slowly into view. *Don't be angry, Mr Harte. I need your help or I'll never get away. I am not joking.*

'Then do not pretend you are Sophie Wade.'

But I am a girl. Do you believe that?

A girl. Until this moment he had been sure this was a boy's prank. But now a doubt crept in. The timid words matched a quiet voice. Perhaps a girl's; but not all girls were quiet. Far from it. But Sophie Wade, a small girl, was as quiet as a mouse, and quieter now where she lay, her large dark eyes quite shut.

'If you are a girl, what is your name?'

The answer caused trouble for the unseen watcher, as he knew it would.

Dear Mr Harte, I wish . . .

The screen had begun writing a letter to him but was unable to think of how to go on. The teacher allowed the watcher to see the thin smile on his lips.

I wish I could convince you that I am who I am.

Anger again got the better of him. 'You are *not* Sophie Wade! She is in hospital. She is unconscious. I have seen her!'

But that can't be me. I am here. It is me who is talking to you! Listen.

'No. I am switching off.' He reached for the button and pressed it. The screen went blank. He pushed his chair back and began to make his way across the dark classroom.

He had taken no more than three steps before the ghost light of the computer lit his way. He spun around. The screen was alive and speaking.

cannot stay awake . . . the mouse . . . I know now . . . try mouse . . . .

The string of dots filled the line and spilled over. They were still chasing each other when he reached the keyboard, but as his fingers touched it the screen faded. He tried to switch on again but nothing happened. He clicked the mouse but it was dead. It was only then that he discovered that the screen should never have come to life in the first place. All evening the computer had been switched off at the wall socket.

Next morning his wife Jean swept away the dark night. 'You were tired,' she said. 'You'd had a long day and then you fell asleep in front of that screen and dreamt it all.'

'But it wasn't even plugged in.'

'You pulled it out while your mind was full of that poor girl.'

She was right, but school was not the same that morning. The corridors were hospital corridors, and the classrooms were wards where everyone's thoughts were on the girl whose life was ebbing away. And there was the unsolved mystery of what had happened to her. All that anyone knew was that she had disappeared only to be found ten days later huddled in the corner of a classroom. She had seemed to be sleeping, but no one had been able to wake her and she was getting weaker.

It was not until mid-morning break that Bob Harte had a chance to get back to the computer. The classroom, however, was not empty. The computers were ranged along one wall and the keyboards were occupied . . . except for the one in the corner.

'You don't want to use that old thing, sir,' said the girl in the next seat. 'It's not much good.' She stood up to offer him her place.

'But you're busy.'

'I've just finished.' Then she saw he was reluctant to change places. 'But some people do like to sit there . . . or used to.' She looked at the ground, not wanting to say any more.

'Who?' he asked.

'Well, there was Sophie,' she said slowly. 'She seemed to like it quite a lot. And she was ever so clever.' But she wasn't happy to be speaking about the girl in hospital so she turned to her friend at the next keyboard. 'She was good, wasn't she?' She reddened. 'I mean Sophie, she *is* good.'

Her friend was not so sensitive. 'She's not as good as some other people, though. Especially one.'

The two girls exchanged glances and seemed about to giggle, but then a shadow crossed their faces as they remembered what had happened to the girl they were talking about. He helped them forget the hospital.

'So it's Sophie's friend who is the good one,' he said. 'How good is she?'

'*He*,' the bolder girl put him right. 'It's Will Smith.' And her eyes rested on him as if just to mention the name explained everything.

Bob Harte did not believe her. Will Smith, tall, boastful, and distant, did not seek anyone's friendship. He was the exact opposite of Sophie Wade, and he was older. 'I wouldn't have thought she was his type,' he said.

'She wasn't,' said the bold one. 'But he was mad on her.'

Dinner duty came as a relief to Bob Harte. He would be too busy to brood. But then, as he collected his pasty and chips from the counter and looked around for a place to sit he saw Will Smith eating alone at an empty table. He sat very upright, meticulously dealing with his food, his attention on nothing else.

'Hi, Will. How's tricks?' Bob could hear himself being the friendly teacher, but Smith had the troubling habit of treating teachers as if he belonged in the staffroom alongside them. His only response was to smile.

'Been doing anything interesting, Will?' Bob busied himself with arranging his plate and cutlery, thinking that only a teacher would choose to sit with this young man. The rest of the noisy crew in the canteen had the good sense to be happy somewhere else. Sophie must have been intimidated by him.

'What did they tell you about me?' said Smith.

The question made the teacher look up sharply. 'Who are you talking about?'

'Those two girls. They're always going on about me and that computer in the corner. They think I'm clever with it. It's embarrassing.'

But he was pleased with himself, and the teacher saw it. It put an idea into Bob Harte's head and when he spoke again he looked down into his plate so that he appeared to be taking little interest. 'But it's just a computer, isn't it? An old one. Even you can't do anything special with it.' He looked up. 'Can you?'

The slate-coloured eyes rested on him with such cool contempt that Bob was sure he was right. He had found the night-time hoaxer. He became more cunning. 'It's just an ancient computer to me,' he said. 'It should be junked.'

And Will Smith laughed and shook his head. 'You're the same as the rest, Mr Harte. It's a machine in a million and you can't see it.'

'So what can it do, Will? Can it talk to you?'

'Talk? I suppose so, maybe. But you still don't understand what I'm saying to you. This isn't the sort of computer you can go into a shop and buy. Every once in a while you find one that has something different internally—it doesn't even know it itself, but it's there if you are smart enough to get right into its depths. And once you tickle it into life it will do things for you.'

'Really,' the teacher murmured and looked around the room as if this boastfulness bored him. Will Smith reacted.

'Listen to me!' Smith's command seemed to echo the first words on the computer screen at night. 'Listen! When a computer begins to tell you its secrets it opens up. It really opens—it lets you inside!'

'Right inside?' Bob chuckled, knowing this would infuriate the pale youth. 'You mean a computer can swallow you up, flesh and bone?'

A grin creased the smooth cheeks. 'Ah, if only you knew what I know, Bob Harte!'

It was insolent, but the teacher let it pass. Smith was heading into deeper trouble than this. But first he had to find out just what madness possessed Smith's mind. 'You certainly impressed those two girls. I think you could convince them that someone could really vanish inside a machine.' He laughed and added, 'Which is ridiculous.'

'Stranger things have happened.'

Smith was smug. He believed he had the teacher baffled, and Bob played along with it. He spoke seriously. 'So you believe it is possible to trap someone inside a machine and hold them prisoner?'

'If you wanted to.'

'But suppose that person found a way out, what then?'

Smith was amused. 'It might not do them much good.'

'Why not?'

And Smith pitied him. 'What you don't understand, Mr Harte, is that the important part—the person's mind—could still be trapped.'

Bob Harte frowned and looked away as if his own mind was grappling with this idea, but he knew he had the hoaxer within his grasp. He sighed and murmured a name to himself. 'Sophie Wade,' he said.

Smith had heard. 'What about her?'

'Nothing. It was merely that what you have just said set me thinking of her lying unconscious in hospital . . . ' Bob broke off and smiled as if the idea embarrassed him. 'I began to wonder if she had been trapped and managed to get away but had left her mind inside the machine.'

Smith spoke sharply. 'What makes you say that?'

'Oh, nothing. Just something that happened to me last night . . . it's of no interest.'

Smith hesitated, but curiosity got the better of him. 'Can't you tell me?'

'I think you already know.' He saw that Smith was puzzled, and went on, 'Your favourite computer was left on last night.' He paused, but Smith showed no reaction. 'Words came on the screen. It spoke to me as though someone was trapped inside.'

Smith frowned at this but still did not admit to being the hoaxer.

'So I tried to find out who it was.' Bob Harte watched him closely. 'But I don't suppose I have to tell you that.'

'Why not?' Smith was still claiming to be ignorant, but the strain showed. He seemed thinner, his cheeks were hollow.

'Because it was you.' The teacher spoke calmly. 'You pretended to be Sophie Wade.'

And Smith tried to laugh. 'It wasn't me and it couldn't be her because she's unconscious.'

'But according to you, Smith, her mind could still be trapped.' Bob looked into the stony face and realized he would never force a confession. He drew a deep breath and surrendered. 'Oh well, I'll give you best this time, Smith. It was a cruel trick, but I have to admit you made a good stab at convincing me you were Sophie Wade last night. I even started doing what Sophie suggested.'

'What was that?'

'She said "try the mouse" and—' He broke off. Smith's face was twisted into an expression he could not understand. 'Are you all right?'

Smith only just managed to nod.

'Well, as you know, because you were somehow watching, I did try the mouse and nothing happened. I don't know how you did it, Smith, but in another minute I'm going to take another look at that computer and see if it talks to me again, mouse or no mouse.'

He got no further. Smith's chair had clattered to the floor and he was gone.

Bob Harte closed his eyes and rubbed his face. He had succeeded. The hoaxer was unmasked and very worried. He yawned and stretched his arms wide.

'He does that to us, too, sir.'

He opened his eyes. There was a group of them, grinning at him.

'He tires us out as well.'

'No one tires me.' He grinned back. 'Who are you talking about?'

'The Mouse, sir. Will Smith.'

They saw his expression change. 'It's because he's so good, sir. He never has to use the mouse, so that's why we call him Mouse . . . '

They scattered as he pushed through them. He was back in a nightmare. The mouse . . . Sophie's last word on the screen as she faded away. His mind raced. Smith and the old computer. He had found a way to use it. Details clicked. Everything held together. Smith had trapped the girl. She had disappeared for ten days and then had escaped—or part of her had. And Smith had not been greatly troubled because he knew that, as long as she was unconscious, her mind was still his, hidden away inside dark machinery, out of the world's reach. But now he had been told that her mind had awakened and had spoken of the Mouse.

Bob Harte knew he had blundered. He had panicked Will Smith and given him time to get to the machine and drag Sophie Wade back to captivity. He ran. He reached the corridor. It was crowded. He caught a glimpse of a fair head at the far end, and a face twisted towards him. If Smith got to the computer before him he would slam the door of Sophie's prison. The fair head vanished in the crowd.

'Mr Harte!' It was the headmaster some distance behind him waving to attract his attention. He waved back and ran on.

No sign of Smith. He reached the classroom. It was dingy, lightless, but through the glass door he saw the glow of a single computer screen. He was in time, Sophie was talking again. But to someone else. He caught a glimpse of a shadowy figure in front of the screen. He crashed into the room and as he did so the screen went dead. And he was alone.

The head came in as he was hammering at the keyboard. 'I can't do it!' he cried. 'I can't make it do anything!'

The head tried to calm him. 'Don't worry about it, Bob. That machine's too old to bother with.' He put himself between Bob and the computer; something else was on his mind. 'I've just had a message from my secretary,' he said. 'It's the hospital. They want to see you at once.' His voice became quieter. 'They didn't say why.'

He found her family at her bedside. Dead? The nurse saw the question in his face and said quietly, 'She's asking to speak to you. She's very weak.'

He went closer. Sophie was very small in the expanse of white sheets. Her eyes opened slowly and rested on him. 'I was a long time in the dark, Mr Harte.' She was speaking directly to him. There was no computer screen between them now. 'I almost got away once,' she said, 'but the Mouse held me back.'

'Then you spoke to me,' he said, 'when the Mouse wasn't there.' He knew this meant nothing to anyone else at the bedside.

'I tried to talk to you again today but you weren't there!'

He nodded. 'I tried, but I got to the classroom too late.'

'I saw the Mouse come in!' Suddenly she sat upright. 'I knew he was coming to lock me away, Mr Harte, so I watched him at the keyboard like I watched you and I saw what keys he used. Then I hit the same keys on my side, and the computer let me out—all of me.'

Her mother, watching and listening, was mystified and frightened by the nonsense her daughter was talking. Bob Harte managed to smile at her and murmured, 'It's all computers . . . we've been working on something.' More would have to be said later. He turned to Sophie. 'So you are free now?' he said. 'Really free?'

She nodded. 'I won't go near that computer. Never. But what if the Mouse comes for me again!'

The nurse came forward and eased Sophie back to her pillow. 'I think we had better stop there,' she said. 'She has to sleep now.'

Will Smith had absented himself from school, and all that Bob Harte could do was to wrench the cable and all the other wires out of the computer's back and jab a screwdriver at its internal workings. He spent a sleepless night, and it was next day before he went back to the classroom. There was a blank space where the old computer had been.

'I had it taken away,' the head told him. 'It was burnt out.' He did not go into explanations because he had other problems on his mind. Another pupil had gone missing.

Will Smith was never seen again.

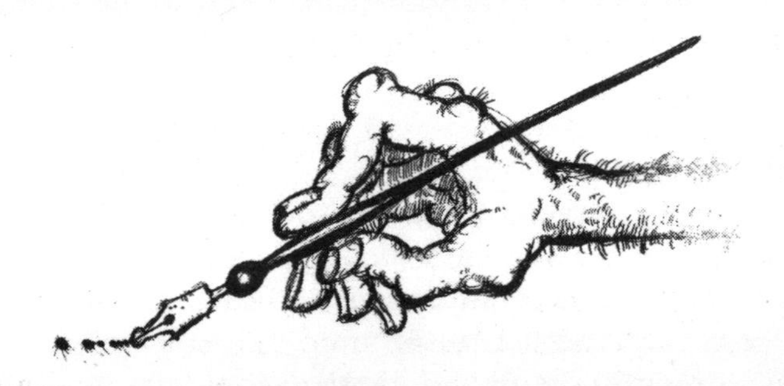

Yesterday Upon the Stair

(*Written in homage to G. K. Chesterton's classic detective, Father Brown*)

DENNIS HAMLEY

'Sir,' said DC Ferguson, our computer whizz. 'Here's another of those e-mails.' He read from the screen: '"*Buster Brady will die between 8 and 12 this morning. Nemo.*"' He looked up. 'He always signs them Nemo,' he said. 'Why?'

'Nemo is Latin for nobody,' I answered.

'I reckon Nemo's this operation's Mr Big,' said DC Murdoch.

'There was an American stand-up comic called Nemo,' said DC Charlotte Crow. 'He was funny. Weird, though.'

'So's this,' said Ferguson.

Ferguson was right. Throughout our hunt for the region's biggest drugs ring, we'd been dogged by Nemo's e-mails. And what Nemo said came to pass. Three murders, none solved. More than weird.

Buster Brady was our prize grass. If he died, we

were finished. I'd found him myself and cultivated him. But, now I was Detective Chief Inspector heading the case, I couldn't consort with grasses like Buster. My underlings looked after him.

'We have to protect him,' said Sergeant Evans.

Buster lived alone in a block of flats near the docks. I rang him. 'You're in danger,' I said. 'Stay put. It's 7.30 a.m. I'm coming to see you.'

We drove to the flats. I climbed the stairs to Buster's and went in. When I returned, Evans asked, 'Is he OK?'

'Fine,' I answered. 'He calmed down when I said he was under surveillance. I checked the flat. No trapdoors, no one hiding in cupboards, all windows locked. Intruders must come through the front door. Evans, Murdoch, you'll watch on the stairs. The rest, stay in the cars, keep watching and miss nothing. Remember Father Brown.'

'Who's he?' asked Charlotte Crow.

'A detective in stories by G. K. Chesterton. There was a murder: everyone swore no one entered the house. Father Brown asked about the postman. We never notice the postman. The invisible man. The postman did it. Watch for the one we never notice.'

'So we arrest the postman?' said Ferguson.

'Only if he acts suspiciously,' I replied. 'We *have* to see somebody, if this Nemo knows something we don't.'

Charlotte Crow spoke. '*Yesterday upon the stair, I met a man who wasn't there, he wasn't there again today, why don't that old man go away?*' She shuddered. 'Nemo,' she said. 'Nobody.'

The mood was tense. 'Right,' I said. 'Let's go.'

But no one came near the flats, not even a postman. 'Quiet as the grave, sir,' said Sergeant Evans when we went in at twelve.

I knocked on Buster's door. 'You can come out now,' I called.

No answer. I unlocked the door. 'Nemo!' Charlotte Crow gasped.

The impossible had happened. Buster was dead, strangled. 'With bare hands,' said the doctor later. 'The murderer must have strong thumbs.'

The Scene of Crime team moved in: we fruitlessly questioned people in the flats. In the evening, we returned to the station. The incident room was quiet. To lighten everyone up, I got bottles of lager in, though it was against the rules. 'Here, cheer up and drink up. We'll crack this case yet,' I said, flicking the tops off with my thumbs and handing bottles round.

'How do you do that, sir?' said DC Murdoch admiringly.

'Just a knack,' I answered.

I let them go soon after. They'd had a bad day. I'd get no useful work out of them now. I'd go off duty myself soon.

Well, well, well. What an interesting day it had been.

In the car park, Charlotte Crow rang her partner on her mobile. 'I'm coming home, Dave,' she said.

'Good,' he answered. 'I'll do a lasagna.'

'Bless you,' said Charlotte.

Curious about what the DCI had said, she called at the library on the way and took out a copy of the Father Brown stories. Then she went to the supermarket. Dave deserved a treat. He usually drank beer in cans, but she saw bottles of German wheat beer on the shelves, said 'Time for a change,' to herself, and bought four.

'What's this rubbish?' said Dave when he saw them.

'You'll like it,' said Charlotte. 'I'll have one too.'

Dave took the tops off with the bottle opener. 'Can't you flick them off with your thumbs?' asked Charlotte.

'No way,' said Dave. 'My thumbs aren't strong enough.'

'My boss can,' said Charlotte, and had an odd thought.

'You're quiet,' said Dave as they ate.

'I've had a bad day,' she answered. 'I'll go to bed early. I'll read for a while.'

'That's OK,' said Dave. 'There's football on telly.'

In bed, she opened her library book and found 'The Invisible Man'. It was written a long time ago. The idea of postmen being invisible struck her as daft. They weren't to her. She knew theirs by his first name. Still, perhaps things were different in those days. But she loved the story. Some bits made her shiver. Warnings of death, sinister laughs heard when nobody seemed near, a murderer in control—until Father Brown sussed him out. She saw what the DCI meant.

And yet, and yet . . . Something worried her.

She woke suddenly at dead of night. She knew what it was. This morning wasn't magic. There *was* an invisible man.

Sinister laughs, death warnings? Of course. Nemo's e-mails.

Her stomach turned over.

Who was in the flat alone with Buster?

Who could flick bottle tops off? Who had strong enough thumbs to strangle a man?

Who was least likely to be the murderer, the Mr Big, *truly* invisible? *Who was Nemo?*

She couldn't sleep again. She held a dreadful secret and didn't know what to do about it.

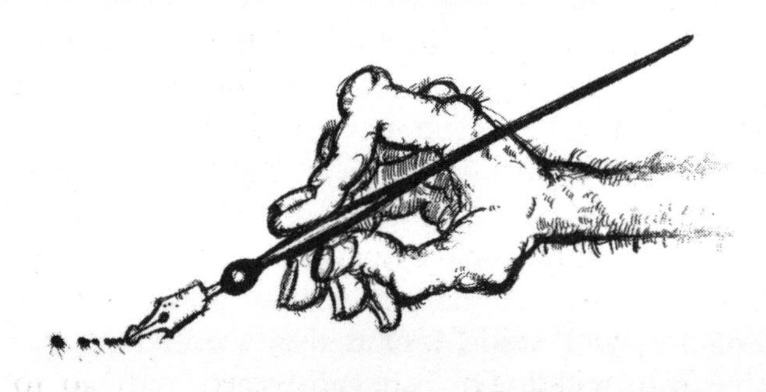

Double Rap

HILARY McKAY

Reach up your arms and press your fingertips hard against a windowpane. Press very hard. So hard that your fingers pull downwards, squeaking against the glass. That's the sound.

There is another sound, too, that I have been hearing all my life. A double rap, like a knock at the door, only sometimes it is on a window, not a door. It comes in the thin, dead hours of the night and it is very loud. Perhaps it sounds so loud because the world is so quiet at that time. The second rap is harder than the first.

When I was little we lived in a cottage in Cumbria that was three hundred years old. All the rooms were dark because the windows were so small and the walls so thick. The back windows of the cottage looked out on to a sort of boggy patch of ground. The front looked across the street to the village church. And the graveyard, of course. The church was not haunted, and neither was the graveyard, nor the boggy patch of ground. You would think they would be, but they were not.

Our cottage was not haunted either, only we did not use the back passage that led from the kitchen to two little rooms like storerooms. It was very cold down there.

The passage ended in a cupboard that went from floor to ceiling, filling the end wall. We did not open the door of that cupboard. I was going to once, I remember how I stood looking at it thinking, Open it and then you will know. But I did not.

I wish I had done now.

Inside that cupboard was a smell, musty and sharp and bitter. It was a smell so strong that when you pressed your nose close you could almost taste it, even with the door closed.

I think my mother must have opened the door sometimes, because the smell would be very intense now and then, all along the passage. One day I asked what was in the cupboard.

'Oh,' said my mother. 'Old baking tins.'

I was too young in those days to have to go to school, and I was so small I could not reach the door-knocker unless I stood on my stool. It was a lovely door-knocker, painted black and shaped like a lion's head. The lion held a ring in its mouth, which was the knocker part. It was very stiff to move. If you wanted to make a loud double rap with that knocker you would have to be strong. I could not do it, except by using both hands and a lot of effort.

When the double rap on that lion door-knocker would come at night I would find myself completely awake all at once, and tingling with anticipation, waiting to hear my mother go downstairs and open the door. I was frightened, too frightened to move or call out, or do anything but listen, but a part of me longed for her to open the door. She never did.

Once, just before we moved away, the double rap woke me and I made myself get out of bed and look. From my bedroom window I could see the quiet churchyard and the church, and the village houses all dark and asleep. I could see our shadowy front garden and the big shells, bone white in the moonlight, that lined the garden path. I could not quite see our front door because of the little porch around it, but I do not think there was anything there. I do not think there was anything unfamiliar anywhere. Not a whisper or a movement. Even the ghost that the whole village knew was not about, the old man in stockings and knickerbockers who appeared in broad daylight, marching along the street and straight through the walls of Mrs Evans's red brick bungalow. Mrs Evans did not mind him at all. She called him 'My brown man' and said he was no trouble. 'I do not think he even notices us,' she said. 'He is just walking home. This bungalow is built right across where the drive to the lodge used to be. He must have lived there once. He does no harm. Even my dogs don't mind him.'

Her dogs minded me. They used to growl at me and walk backwards with stiff legs. I do not like dogs, and I did not like Mrs Evans. Just before we decided to move she told my mother she could not have me coming round any more. I did not care. Anyway, she would never tell me properly about her ghost. She used to try and talk to me about dogs and aeroplanes and treasure hunting and stuff like that and she got mad when I walked away. And she was wrong about the brown man. Even if he did not notice her he definitely noticed me. I saw him turn his head and look at me once.

Anyway, he was not there that night the double rap

came and I looked out of my bedroom window, just before we moved away.

My mother liked moving house. She was a painter, and she liked new places to paint. After Cumbria we went to the borders of Scotland, to a basement flat in a big old house on the banks of the river Tweed. There were pine woods all about, and a village school not too far away.

'You can make friends here,' said my mother. 'You can bring them home and go exploring with them.'

I did not make any friends. Anyway, I liked exploring on my own. I found a little door that led under the Big House to the cellars. They were low and musty, like stone caves, with huge shelves where barrels of beer once stood, and empty wine racks and great damp curtains of cobwebs looping everywhere. I did not go there very often.

Yes I did.

I had been sorry to leave the cottage in Cumbria, with the cupboard and the lion knocker, but now I had the cellars. The cellar roof was very low, and the ground was so damp there were puddles on the floor. Between the puddles the ground was chalky, and palely muddy. There were a lot of footprints in the pale chalk mud but I think they were all mine.

The double rap had come with us when we moved.

When we lived in the basement flat the double rap came at the kitchen window, not the front door. It was an old-fashioned window, the sort that slides up and down, but it would not open. It was stuck shut with layers and layers of paint. I tried to pick them off, but I could not. The double rap came very loudly in that basement flat, rattling the glass in the kitchen window, but I never got there in time.

I thought there might be something in the woods

and the back of the house because they were so dark, and on windy nights the trees whistled and creaked and seemed to press closer together. Also I knew there was something strange about because there were other people with flats in the big house and I had heard two of the women talking. They had their heads close together but I clearly heard one of them say, 'There's something very strange about h—'

Then they caught sight of me and jumped and shut up.

A man lived in a little house in the woods. He was always about. He had a pole he called a vermin pole, and it had dead animals, rats and moles and rooks and a jay hung on it. The man cut trees and made them into fence posts and things like that. The odd bits of tree left over he used to cut up for firewood logs. He had a very sharp saw called a circular saw that he used for making his logs. One day, when I came up behind him suddenly, he cut himself on this saw. I said, 'What is there round here?'

He was very unfriendly and snapped, 'What do you mean, what is there?' and he looked at my hands and feet as if they were strange and disgusting to him. I remember they were white and chalky with mud from the cellars.

'Ghosts,' I said. 'And haunted places.'

He was throwing the logs as he cut them on to a big heap. He began throwing them quite hard. The blood from where he had cut himself made a mark on each log.

'You're the only thing that haunts round here,' he said, very grumpily. 'What you been doing to get like that? Prowling about them cellars?'

I did not answer, I just looked at his hand, still bleeding.

'How old are you, then?' he asked.

'Eleven,' I said.

'Boy your age should have better to do,' he said, still throwing logs. 'You should be thinking of football, not ghosts. You should be off with your mates.'

I went to look at his vermin pole to see if he had got any more. He didn't like that either.

'Get off with you and do something natural,' he shouted.

He thought I went away, but I didn't. I just moved where he couldn't see me. I stayed a long time, watching him cut and throw the logs. He kept looking over his shoulder and his hand kept bleeding all the while. One day not long after that his old tractor that he used for pulling the felled trees out of the wood tipped over and rolled over while he was driving. Its engine ran for a while, and then stopped. He died underneath it.

Afterwards I used to go and look at the place.

What is everyone so frightened of? I have looked and looked. I have listened and watched and waited. There is nothing.

My mother said, 'We are moving again. That school is not a success and this place is making you worse. I thought a nice, rough and tumble village school . . . Please look at me when I am talking to you.'

Then after a bit she said, 'I wish you would not stare at me like that.'

So we moved for a third time. This time to a town, although my mother did not like living in towns. I know why she chose it though. It was because there was a school nearby where you boarded all week and came home for weekends. She bought me new pyjamas and a football kit and a skateboard and a book of jokes and she made me go there.

I could hardly hear my double rap in that place. It was never quiet enough. Now and then I caught it though, bump bumping softly on the bedroom window.

The boys at this school thought they were tough. I expect they would have been approved of by the dead man in the woods. They liked football, for instance.

Football did not help them much in the middle of the night.

'What are you afraid of?' I asked them. 'Is it the knocking? Is it the knocking?'

The boys at that school were very easily frightened. Terrified. Shaking even, some of them.

After a few weeks the school sent me home.

My mother is still pretending she cannot hear the knocks but I notice she has taken to locking her bedroom door at night.

Bang, bang, they go, every night now. A double rap in the thin dead hours of the dark. Ferocious on the front door, thunderous on my bedroom window. I fall asleep knowing it will come, and wake up to find myself not in bed. I am at the bedroom window, and my arms are reached up high, and my hands are against the cold glass, pressing hard. I am pressing very hard, and pulling my hands down as I press, so that my fingertips screech on the glass.

That is the sound that wakes me, that screech.

Before long whatever is out there will get in.

Or I shall get out.

Very soon one of these things will happen.

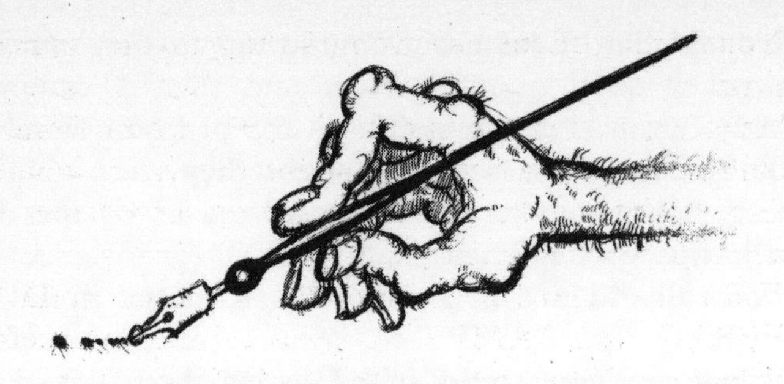

Maggie's Window

MARJORIE DARKE

Edith gave a sudden shout: 'Police!'

Uniformed men surged out, surrounding them. In the struggle, shopping bags were kicked aside. Muriel's hat was knocked off and trodden underfoot. More people joined the watching crowd. Maggie saw Una being handcuffed, then a flash of sunlight from the spike of Dad's helmet as he turned, raising his thumb.

'We've got 'em this time,' he called—and she saw Una look back at her with dawning understanding that turned to intense sad disappointment.

But Maggie hadn't betrayed them, for all her father had wanted her to. It had to be someone else.

She often looked back to that day, remembering everything that happened from the moment she first met her new companions.

It was raining cats and dogs and blowing a gale as Maggie came out of school. As she crossed the street, the wind scooped up a soggy piece of newspaper and plastered it against her skirt.

'You joining them bad women then, Mag?' someone shouted.

Maggie glared at the bunch of giggling girls from her school running away down the street. What bad women?

Rain trickled down her neck and the newspaper was so wet it peeled off in strips.

'WIN . . . ASH . . . LONDON . . . EST END . . . SUFFRAG . . . RAMP . . . ' was all that was left of the headlines. She rolled it into a ball and flicked the squashy mess into the gutter. Who cared what went on in London? It was like a thousand miles away. They were probably all mad and bad there.

The rain was sheeting down now. By the time she turned into the street where she lived, her boots had leaked, wetting her stockings. She went up the entry between her house and the next. Opening the door into the kitchen she heard Mam call:

'That you, our Mag? Leave your boots on, duck. I want you to take this round for me.' She came into the kitchen with a packet in her hand.

'Oh, Mam, do I have to? I'm soaked.'

'I promised the blouse would be ready today. Paradise Street, number 15. I've wrapped it in oilcloth. Hurry up. I'll have your tea and dry clothes ready for when you get back.'

Maggie scowled, but took the packet and went out.

'Bring that oilcloth back, mind!' Mam called.

Sloshing through puddles gleaming under the gaslamps, Maggie felt as if she was in the wash tub—clothes soaked through to her vest and bloomers. The windows of the terraced houses in Paradise Street cried tears of rain. Number fifteen had light coming through thin drawn curtains. Maggie banged the knocker.

A long pause.

Losing her temper she began to bang even louder.

Before she could let go, the door opened and she almost overbalanced. A face peered out.

'Yes?'

Maggie recognized the narrow green eyes and plump cheeks—Cora Carter! Not so long ago they both went to St Luke's Elementary, though Cora had been in the top class. A bossy sneak of a girl, always ready to tell on you. Maggie thrust the packet towards her.

'Mam said to bring this round—and she wants the oilcloth back.' She was too fed up to care if she sounded rude.

The face retreated and there was a murmur of conversation, followed by rustling. Then the door reopened.

'You'd better come in.' Cora didn't sound welcoming.

Maggie stepped straight into a small living room where three women sat around a table. Light shone from a wall gas-mantle. The table had a cloth flung untidily over it. Underneath, not quite hidden, was what looked like a strip of the calico Mam used to stiffen anything from cushion covers to jackets. Maggie saw the painted letters 'VOTES FO' in green but the rest disappeared under the cloth. On the floor, as if plonked down in a rush, were some pots of paint and brushes.

'Maggie Burton, isn't it?' Cora said. 'I remember you were always in hot water at school.'

'I wouldn't mind some hot water now. I'm freezing.' Maggie hadn't meant to joke and the sudden laughter made her feel silly.

'Put the kettle on for some tea, Edith,' one of the women said. 'We all need warming.'

Edith, big and bony, jumped up, kicking over a pot of green paint with one large foot. A brush shot on to the cloth and paint splashed both calico and the older woman's shoes.

'I'm so sorry, Muriel. All our work for nothing. The lettering is ruined . . . what a blithering idiot!'

'Never mind that.' Muriel patted her grey bun of hair, with a warning glance towards Maggie. 'See to your friend, Cora.'

Cora frowned and flushed. Unwrapping the wet oilcloth she shoved it at Maggie. 'Tell your mam I'll be round Friday with the money.'

An awkwardness filled the room. The third woman, a skinny red-head with a snub nose, fetched cloths and a basin of water. Mopping the floor, she gave Maggie a quick smile. There was no offer of tea, but Maggie was only too glad to escape into the street, despite the sleet.

Once home, she changed and wolfed down the sausages and mash left in the oven to keep warm. Her dad, back from his shift at the station, was toasting his feet on the fender as he read his newspaper. He turned a page and shook it.

Maggie saw the headlines . . .

'MASS WINDOW SMASHING IN LONDON'S WEST END. SUFFRAGETTES ON THE RAMPAGE!' So that's what her schoolmates were on about!

'What's Suffragettes, Dad?'

'Eh?' He looked to see what she had been reading. 'Oh, them! A bunch of loonies. Nothing worth bothering with. Pour us some more tea, duck.'

She did as he asked and passed him his cup. 'What do they do?'

'What do who do?' Mam asked, coming downstairs.

Maggie pointed to the newspaper headline.

'Crack-brained women as want their heads looking at!' Mam said with a disapproving sniff. 'Breaking folk's windows . . . burning buildings. All for some daft notion about being like men so as they can vote who goes to Parliament.'

Hearing 'VOTE' was like a firecracker going off. Big green letters seemed to dance in the air in front of Maggie's eyes. Cora and those others with their calico and pots of paint—were they Suffragettes?

Mam was still talking. 'They'll end up in jug, the lot of 'em, and good riddance!' She began to clear the table. 'Where's the money for the blouse, our Mag?'

'What?' Maggie's mind was still darting about, trying to make sense of what she had seen.

'The money,' Mam said impatiently.

'Oh . . . says she'll bring it round Friday.'

Not pleased, Mam stumped into the kitchen.

'Dad,' Maggie tried to sound casual, 'are there Suffragettes in our town?'

He looked over his newspaper. 'Some—we haven't managed to nab 'em yet. About their daftest trick was painting VOTES FOR WOMEN on a golf course green.' He winked at her. 'Not thinking of joining 'em are you?'

She knew it was a joke but went very red.

'What's up with you?' he asked.

'Only thinking,' she said, redder than ever.

'Well if it's about anything I should know, promise you'll tell me, won't you?' For a moment he sounded serious.

'Course—I'm not stupid!'

'That's my lass!' He chuckled and went back to his paper.

In bed Maggie tossed and turned. When she did drop into a restless sleep, she dreamed of Cora and the other women. Under the purring gaslight, they were madly painting VOTE VOTE VOTE over tablecloth, carpet, walls, ceiling, even their own clothes. Everything was plastered with green paint.

She woke sweating, and thought—when Cora brings the money round I'll find out if they are Suffragettes. A thrill of nervous excitement prickled down her arms as a hazy plan began to form.

Ask to join them . . . worm my way in . . . tell Dad like he asked . . . then just maybe, we could catch them.

Her mind made up, she felt more settled and fell asleep.

In daylight, her plan seemed full of holes. First off, Cora would look down her weaselly nose and say they didn't take school kids.

Out of bed, Maggie glanced in her mirror. She was big for her age. Bigger than Cora, and her face wasn't so fat—altogether she looked more grown-up. No one would ask how old she was, would they? But as she ate her breakfast she began to feel jittery.

Towards the end of a restless week she was bored with waiting. After school on Thursday she caught a glimpse of Cora turning into the street where the police station was and for a moment thought of running to catch her up. But what was there to say? Friday came. She was still lost in trying to decide what to do when her arm was nudged and she almost leapt into the gutter.

'Excuse me, Maggie, isn't it?'

Maggie nodded, recognizing the skinny red-head who had mopped up the spilled paint. She was loaded with canvas shopping bags.

'A bit of luck seeing you. I was on the way to your house. Poor old Cora has gone and sprained her ankle. It's bound up and she's having to hobble with a stick, so I promised to call round with the money for your ma.' Putting down her bags she rummaged in her purse.

'When did she do that?' Maggie asked.

'Wednesday, she said. Fell downstairs, poor thing.' She held out an envelope. 'Here you are. You don't mind taking it, do you? Only I'm late for the meeting.' The twinkling smile Maggie remembered lit up her face. 'Muriel can be quite snappy to latecomers!'

Maggie was on the point of saying: 'But I saw Cora yesterday teatime and she wasn't hobbling.' But she held her tongue. Whatever the day, this was a piece of luck! She could take Cora's place. 'Is it a Suffragette meeting you're off to, miss?' she asked and saw the startled glance.

'It's Mrs actually—Mrs Wren—but call me Una, everyone does!' The bright blue eyes studied Maggie as if trying to make up her mind whether she was to be trusted. 'Why do you want to know?'

'I'd like to join,' Maggie said boldly.

'Didn't Cora say you were still at school?'

'I've left.' A white lie. It would be true in a few weeks. 'If Cora's laid up, perhaps I can help out. I'm good at sewing and painting.' She didn't know what had made her say that.

Una looked at her doubtfully. 'Are you sure your mother won't wonder where you are and worry?'

'No.' Mam would think she had stayed behind at school, but to say so would admit to lying. 'Can I help carry something?'

'Thanks.' Una handed her a bag and shivered. 'This wind is like knives! Come on—we must hurry.'

Maggie let go the breath she had been holding. She was over the first obstacle!

The Friday evening shoppers were thinning out so it was not difficult to keep up a good pace, though the bag was heavy and knocked against her legs with a chinking sound. They left the High Street and hurried past the wool factory, then a huddle of shops. In less than ten minutes they were in a road of larger houses with bay windows and small front gardens. Una opened an iron gate, went to the front door and pulled the bell. A maid opened the door and stood back to let them enter.

Una took off her coat and made Maggie do the same, handing them to the maid. 'Thank you, Sarah. We will see ourselves in.' Leaving most of her shopping in the hall, she took the bag from Maggie and led her into a room stuffed with heavy furniture. Two women were sitting on a sofa by a blazing fire. Edith, who had kicked over the paint, and the grey-haired Muriel.

'At last!' Muriel got up, eyeing Maggie. 'We thought you weren't coming, Una. Where's Cora?'

'Sorry to be so late.' Una apologized, and explained what had happened. 'I'd have been later still if it hadn't been for Maggie here. We met by accident and as she is keen to join I brought her along . . . all hands to the plough!'

Maggie felt a sudden tension in the room.

Muriel said: 'Always glad of new recruits . . . but this is hardly the right time.'

Una blushed as if she had been scolded. 'We could have done with more supporters even before Cora wrecked her ankle.'

'There are still us three,' Edith said.

'Hardly a bold demonstration,' Muriel pointed out. 'We should postpone it.'

'And fail to support our London sisters?' Una sounded shocked. 'You can't mean that, Muriel. Cora gave me the chains.'

'And I've brought the padlocks,' Edith added. 'It does seem a shame to waste all our planning.'

'I suppose we could make a stand,' Muriel said reluctantly. 'But it's hardly fair to ask such a new recruit to take part.'

There was an exchange of glances. As if the three were talking without words.

Having got this far Maggie was desperate to be accepted. 'I'm very strong,' she said quickly. 'Stronger than Cora. I could stand in for her. Just tell me what I must do.'

Another wordless conversation. Muriel relented.

'Very well. But on one condition—that you shall not be chained.' She looked at Una and Edith. 'Agreed?'

'We need a beast of burden,' Edith said.

'And a lookout,' Una added with a wink.

Maggie beamed. They might have been talking double Dutch, but she didn't care. She'd been accepted!

'I'll ring for some tea,' Muriel said. 'After that we'll finish the banner and go over final plans.'

That night, Maggie lay awake, hounded by guilt. She really had meant to tell Dad about what was to happen tomorrow. But thinking of those women, the words had stuck in her throat. The trouble was they liked her, trusted her . . . more than that, what they believed in was *right*. Women *should* be able to vote. Why shouldn't they be as good as men?

Turning over she punched the pillow, which seemed full of stones.

How could she betray them? But if she didn't, then she'd betray her own father. Oh, what should she do? The guilt grew worse, chasing through her dreams when finally she dozed off in the small hours.

* * *

Saturday dawned bright and cold, with a piercing wind. Maggie got out of bed feeling nervous. Today was The Day! Knowing that at all costs she must not let Mam guess what she was up to, she forced down some porridge and tea, but couldn't face toast. Dad had already left for work, which was a relief. What she had to do was carry on as planned—not get cold feet and rock the boat. She washed up the breakfast pots quickly and put on coat and scarf then called upstairs:

'Going out, Mam. I need more tape to mend my school apron,' and escaped into the street.

The arrangement was to meet up at Muriel's house. From there they'd walk together—four ordinary people going to the shops.

'That way we won't attract attention until we are ready,' Muriel had explained.

All the same, Maggie's pulse was racing as she waited for the front door to open. Una answered her knock and smiled at her.

'There . . . I told Muriel we could rely on you. We're all ready. Carry this will you?' She handed Maggie a rolled parcel.

Taking it, Maggie felt a squirm of guilt, remembering how near she had come to letting the cat out of the bag. But that was over. She was a real Suffragette now and they could depend on her.

They walked in twos, each with a shopping bag—Una with Maggie behind Muriel and Edith. The distance from Muriel's house to the Town Hall Square was less than a mile but felt more like twenty. As they walked along the pavement Maggie glanced down at her sensible brown coat, brown skirt and boots, feeling as if she were dressed in scarlet and orange. Everyone must be looking at her. But a cart passed, followed by a couple of traps, then several people on foot. Nobody took any notice.

A church clock struck half past ten as they arrived in the Town Hall Square. The Town Hall was a big Victorian red brick building with railings in front and, curving up either side, steps leading to double doors. These doors were closed. Several people were about, but no one gave them more than a glance as they paused, apparently for a chat.

'You each know what to do,' Muriel said in her fussy way. 'Unroll the banner, Maggie, while we chain ourselves to the railings . . . Una, you haven't forgotten the stones?'

'Of course not!' Una patted her bag. 'Nor my chain and padlock.' Her smile twinkled and included Maggie who glanced away towards the nearest window which looked back at her like a blind eye. Heart thumping, she began to unwrap the parcel with fingers that seemed to have doubled in size.

'Let me give you a hand,' Una offered.

'No!' Maggie hadn't meant to snap.

Una gently squeezed her arm, whispering: 'Brave girl.'

A few people had stopped to stare as string and paper fell to the ground. The banner Maggie had helped to repaint with VOTES FOR WOMEN! was to be tied to the railings on the opposite side of the steps. She had sewn on the strings herself. As the others produced their chains and began to wind them through the railings and then round themselves, time seemed to stretch out endlessly. Anxiously, Maggie's gaze swept the Square, the Town Hall windows, returning to the main doors just as they began to open.

Edith gave a sudden shout: '*Police!*'

* * *

Maggie wanted to call out: 'It wasn't me as told on you!' but they'd never believe her. Seeing the women so roughly handled, she felt a helpless anger with Dad for setting up this ambush. But how had he known? Had she talked in her sleep? The anger turned on herself—somehow she had betrayed her friends.

At that instant she glanced at the growing crowd and felt as if she had been punched. *Cora* was there, watching. No stick. No bound-up ankle. Her green eyes squeezed up in a smug smile as she spotted Maggie and waved. Everything fell into place. Cora resenting Muriel telling her what to do; Cora walking easily towards the police station last Thursday; Cora here, gloating. Cora the spy! Indignation flooded through Maggie, followed by bitter shame. They were both traitors. *And Dad had planned all this without breathing a word.*

Anger swelled.

The women were being hustled up into the Town Hall. Una ignored her, but Muriel and Edith had seen Cora and glanced from her back to Maggie. Their dismay came like a hard slap.

A stone from Una's bag had rolled into the gutter where it lay, seeming to beckon. Maggie picked it up, feeling its smooth weight . . . then, with all her strength, hurled it through the nearest Town Hall window. The tinkling crash filled her with joy. The banner had been taken, but she shouted at the top of her voice:

'VOTES FOR WOMEN! VOTES FOR WOMEN!' and trembling with fright, leaned against the railings, waiting for the handcuffs.

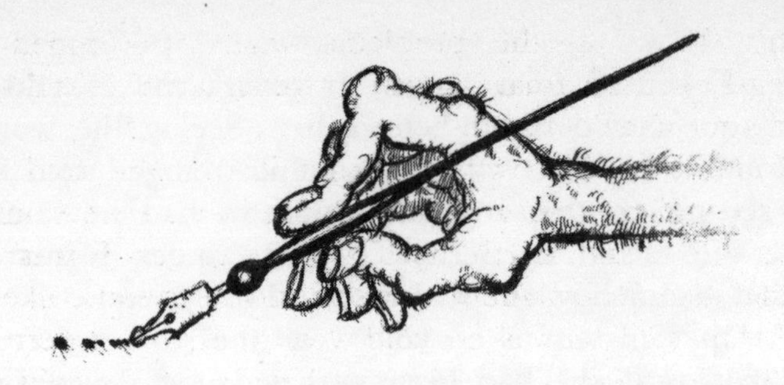

Earth 23

ROBERT DAWSON

Lucy went missing first. One minute she was there beside me and the next she had gone. She turned up a few moments later in the corridor outside the classroom where we had our school lessons, as if she'd passed through the partition.

'How did you get there?' I asked.

'How d'you think?' she snapped. 'What're you on about?'

'One minute you were by me, the next out there!' I protested. 'That's what I mean.'

She tapped her head. 'You're daft!' She softened, 'It's the cold I expect. It's brought on another of your . . . ' She didn't need to say any more. You could almost slice the contempt in her voice and use it to garnish pizzas.

I didn't say anything more. Not then. Not even to Mum. Being in charge of the expedition I reckoned she had enough on her mind. It hadn't been easy. Five years on the spacecraft with all the squabbling and arguing to sort out, and little Geoff being born on the flight. Then all the problems when we landed on E23—Earth 23 that is—the twenty-third Earth-like planet to be discovered.

Mum and Dad would've said it was the cold too, and the old trouble. I mean, I couldn't remember much about what the Earth itself was like, cos I was too young. But I remember the sun, and it wasn't like on E23. On E23 it was so cold you hardly ever left the settlement; so cold it made your head ache. As cold as a judge. No, that's not right—yes, as cold as ice, that's it. Well, obviously.

Later on in the evening when Lucy went, I was playing with Geoff to tire him out before his bedtime when he disappeared, too. We were playing one of his stupid snap games—the astronomy one, with the stars and planets and galaxies and what not. I was losing. Well, I had to or dear Geoff would have thrown a wobbler and *never* gone to sleep.

'Snap!' he said when I very slowly put down a second Milky Way.

To be honest, I wasn't concentrating. My mind was on other things and I had a headache. I played another card—and he wasn't there.

'Geoff?' I said. 'Stop mucking about! Where are you?'

I looked under the mess table, but he wasn't there. Not even Geoff'd try to hide under a glass-topped and tubular-steel-legged table.

But he *wasn't* there! Really! I found him in the settlement kitchen, wrapped round a reconstituted marmalade and ryebread sandwich and sipping a glass of milk.

No, of course we didn't have cows. It was milk powder mixed with water. After all, that was the one thing the planet had—masses of water, more than you could ever imagine, even though it was all frozen. As frozen as . . . as—E23.

Mum smiled at me. 'All right now, dear?' she asked. It wasn't me, it was Geoff.

'What're you doing in here?' I asked him. She should have asked Geoff, him vanishing like that.

'Making a sandwich,' he said. Only his mouth was so stuffed it came out as 'mmmmmming a snnnnch,' and white milk spurted out of the corners of his mouth.

'I mean,' I asked, 'how did you disappear?'

'You zonked out and I was bored,' he replied, as if it was the most natural thing in the world. 'You weren't playing properly. You were letting me win.'

I nearly denied it. But I didn't want an argument. I just wanted him out of the way. This thing about people disappearing and appearing somewhere else was getting worrying.

Next day at breakfast, I snapped at Geoff for singing because he wasn't—singing nicely I mean. Dad shouted at me for making Geoff cry. It was the headache made me grumpy. I shouldn't have been. But Dad shouldn't have been so nasty. I'm not always as bad-tempered as a carrot. No, I've got that wrong. Bad-tempered as a bull, I think he said.

Then Dad vanished. I'd watched him leave the settlement to walk over to the nearest hill. For once, it wasn't snowing, and the morning was clear. It wasn't a school day, and Mum suggested we go sledging down the hill opposite. But to be honest, that's all we'd done for five years—sledging or throwing snowballs or making snow houses, day after day. And it gets boring, especially when the snow house you made two years ago is still there, bulging under the next layer of snow. Boring. As boring as a screwdriver. So I stayed in and chatted whilst Mum wrote the settlement log for yesterday.

'I wish they'd hurry up and explode that nuclear device,' I said. 'There used to be sunshine on Earth! I can remember. It was warm and sort of bright and colourful. Not like here. Grey white, grey blue. Everywhere. As dull as a dredger, as ditchwater.'

'The settlement isn't!' she defended, scribbling away. 'It was designed with lots of bright colours! And anyway, there's no guarantee that a nuclear device will change E23's orbit or adjust the tilt!'

'I'm sure it will! It can't make it worse! Wouldn't having summer be great! Spring, summer, autumn, winter, instead of winter always.'

'Don't be silly. There are seasons here already. We're well into spring, and the supply ship with the next group of scientific settlers will be here in the autumn.'

I watched Dad trudging through the snow towards the top of the hill, and the weather station we'd erected.

Suddenly, as suddenly as Lucy and Geoff had appeared, there was a man in front of Dad. A huge man. Dad's no midget but I reckon this man was two and a half metres tall. Dad stopped in his tracks. I saw him look up at the man's face and speak. The man answered.

'Mum!' I pointed. 'Look! There's a man there! But there can't be! It's uninhabited except for us.'

'You're seeing things!' Mum said.

Then Dad vanished. But the tall man didn't.

'Dad's disappeared!' I almost shouted. 'Look!'

This time, Mum did look up. But as she did, the tall man disappeared too!

'Dad must have gone to the other side of the hill,' she said. 'That's all.'

'He didn't!' I protested. 'Something's happened. There was a tall man there! I told you!'

'We're the only people here,' Mum said calmly. 'All the advance probes prove it. You've probably had one of your turns. E23 was chosen because it was uninhabited. A young planet just emerging from its first ice age, so we could get the detailed data. The only living things out there are microbes and bacteria, and not many of them!'

'Then where's Dad?' I insisted. 'I'm going to look for him.'

Mum sighed, but all she said was, 'Keep in sight of the settlement.'

I followed Dad's footsteps all the way up the hill to where he'd gone. The footsteps stopped there. They didn't come back. There was no sign of the tall man, or Dad. I'd half hoped he might have fallen under the snow, but he hadn't. The snow was pure white, untouched, as pure as honey, except for the footprints. But only Dad's.

'Dad!' I wailed. 'Dad!'

There was no answer.

I was scared now. It's against scientific fact, footprints which stop suddenly. No Dad! No sign! As if he'd been plucked from the planet surface.

And I thought I understood. Dad had been snatched by the tall man, in some sort of spacecraft which I hadn't seen. It was the only possible explanation.

'Dad!' I called again. 'Where are you?'

I started crying. Well, it was six years ago now, and I was only ten. You'd have cried too, if your dad had suddenly disappeared.

Crying wasn't a very good idea. The tears froze as they dripped, and I imagined all the new species of bacteria falling into the snow to thaw out after the nuclear explosion. A bit of me, really.

'Dad!' I was almost screaming it now.

In desperation, I turned to look down at the settlement. The lights were on in the main mess, and I could see several of my school friends. They were all waving madly at me.

I waved back, out of politeness, but really I wished they'd understand my panic over Dad, them waving like demented trees.

Then I saw someone walking towards me up the hill. It was Devon's dad, striding through the snow, following the footprints Dad and I had left. When he got near enough he shouted.

'Your dad's fine! He's at the settlement.'

I didn't understand that. He couldn't possibly have gone back without me seeing him. I trudged down the hill.

It was true! Dad was there! He'd come back from the hill. He had a bad headache and he'd had one of his fits, so he went for a lie down on his bunk. I went to see him to ask if he really was OK and about the tall man.

'Sure, I'm fine,' he said. 'Except for the headache with the cold.'

'So if you're fine, how did you get back to the settlement? I was watching you all the time.'

'I walked, of course.'

But he couldn't have. I'm not blind. And if I'd zonked out he'd have stayed with me, to make sure I was OK.

'I was watching you all the time. Then a tall man came in front of you. Who was he?'

Dad looked puzzled. 'I never saw one. There was only you there!'

'What?' I protested.

'You and me. You can't have forgotten. Then I went back. I left you there. I knew you'd be all right with your extra thermal.'

That wasn't what happened, but then I realized. It was the tall man who'd made Dad forget.

'You talked to him. I saw you!'

'Did I? No, it's the cold. It's playing tricks. My head hurts. It's pounding.'

'Dad, this is important. You disappeared, then the tall man did. I was watching from the settlement. What happened?'

Dad groaned and held his forehead. 'I told you, I walked and you stayed.'

'I know your head hurts, but do you actually remember walking?'

Dad nursed his head. 'At the minute, I can't remember anything, except how much my head hurts. It's a cold head again. Even with all the protective headgear, this cold seems to eat through everything. I'm not surprised there's nothing alive here.'

'But there is, Dad. The tall man! And something is going on. You disappeared. Honest! You turned up here. Geoff disappeared yesterday and so did Lucy.'

Dad groaned. 'It's the cold. It does things to you. Now do me a favour, disappear yourself will you, so I can have a sleep?'

That evening, a group of us were playing Monoplanet. It's like Monopoly only with stars and planets instead of roads. There was me, Lucy, Devon Junior, and Purnima. Purnima's dad—he's the electronics engineer—came through the general mess room and stood by me to watch the game. But not just him—there was a tall man as well. Only no one else seemed to notice. Actually, it was off-putting. I'd just landed in the Sirius Solar System and was building a full civilization, which you can't do by the rules until you've had a settlement colony first. I knew that, of course.

'He's cheating,' Purnima's dad announced. Luckily the others didn't hear.

Me! I ask you! Who knows the rules inside out. Point is, they didn't, which was why I was getting away with it till he came.

It made me mad. It was our game, he had no right to stick his ear in. Do I mean ear? Something like that. I wished he was somewhere else.

And he was! I mean, he wasn't there any more.

Now don't get me wrong. I know I said wished. But it wasn't magic or anything stupid like that. There was no magic wand. Really, it was the tall man. And the others didn't realize. I couldn't say anything about him going suddenly or they'd have realized I was cheating. Well, not cheating—playing to win, which I did in the end.

Next day, Lucy went missing again. We were doing Interstellar Geography and, as usual, she was big headed and said she knew better than me. I was doing my special work at the time. It was nothing to do with her.

I admit I wasn't sorry, because if she'd stayed around much longer I might have sloshed her. Suddenly, she disappeared. So did the tall man who'd been standing behind her.

It was three hours before I found her in the fruit garden, eating grapes. Oh, that—it's like a big heated greenhouse really, so we can get some fresh food. Could get.

'I've only just come!' she wailed.

I thought, Oh no you haven't, Lucy Liar. Three hours you've been in here. I bet you stuffed yourself. At any rate, there was a load of pineapples gone, and no one admitting to it!

'Pull the other one!' I said, and pointed to the

pineapple peel all over the floor, and the tall man in the corner.

She looked at me as if she couldn't understand what I was on about and that showed she was pretending to be innocent.

'*You* did that,' she said at last.

I giggled. It was such a stupid lie. 'The cold's getting to you!' I said. 'You need to see the doc!'

After that, people began disappearing regularly. But oddly, it was only me that ever saw it happen. Usually they just went. Always one of the tall men was nearby at the time.

Yes, they were always around. Everywhere I went. I knew then, of course. It was me they were interested in. They'd seen something special in me. I'd worked it all out by that time. They were able to disappear at will and could cause us to, as well, when they wanted to.

One day, I asked one, 'Why don't you ever make me disappear and appear somewhere else?'

'Because you're special,' he answered.

Which made me think. 'Go on then, if I'm special, do it to me, so I can find out what it's like.'

I stood there for what seemed an age whilst the tall man looked at me. His eyes were sharp brown, and made my head ache. I don't know how long I stood there, or didn't. But suddenly I realized I *was* somewhere else, in another room, and it was an hour later.

That was the first time it happened to me, and the last (I think). But once, just before the supply ship came in the autumn (Ha-ha!—winter really, of course) I was out skating on a piece of ice when Mum came charging up with Dad and two or three others.

'Oh, thank God, thank God,' she cried, and snatched me into her arms. She hugged me and squeezed me. I didn't get it at first. 'Thank God you're all right,' she said.

'Course I am, why shouldn't I be?'

'But you just disappeared. We didn't know where you were!' she said.

'I didn't!' I protested. 'I've been here, skating.'

'You know the rules, you never go anywhere without telling someone first, and you always stay in sight of the settlement. In all this cold, it's too dangerous.'

But I knew I hadn't disappeared, because I knew where I was. And the tall man knew too, because he'd been standing watching me most of the time. I guess he must've brought me here. So perhaps, to Mum and that lot, I *had* vanished.

Lucy disappeared two days later. We had this big argument when she told me I'd got the maths wrong again, and I really wished she'd get lost.

Which she must have. Unless it was the tall men took her. She just vanished.

They found her two days later on the hill by the weather station. Poor Lucy, in those night temperatures she'd frozen despite the thermal suit.

What I couldn't remember was why she hadn't gone back to the settlement with me. Maybe it was the tall man. It was no more than a cock's toe—I mean cock's crow, cock's stride—from the settlement. I ought to know, the number of times I've been there. Which is what I said to everyone.

People looked at me a bit funny after that. When the supply ship came with the next batch of people, Mum and Dad decided I ought to go back to Earth for some specialized treatment, which I didn't need. Dad came with me because of his awful headaches, like mine.

* * *

So here I am back with you.

The doctors here on proper Earth say that all this people disappearing and reappearing is in my mind. Failing to relate to the real world—that's their words. An effect of the cold, I suppose. All that sledging and snowballing when we first got there. Damaged something in the brain, I expect. They say I don't understand what's going on.

That's nonsense, and I can prove it to you in a minute. You don't get to sixteen and spend ten years going to and fro in space without learning a lot. I ought to know. It's my brain, after all, I'm as normal as a judge. No, wait a minute, there's something wrong there. I'm as sober as a judge—I mean, as sober as a cucumber.

Anyway, I said I can prove it. When I say NOW stop reading this and look across to the far side of the room.

NOW!

Well? Did you see me? Standing with my back to the wall? In the silvery suit? Next to the tall man? Yes, I thought you would.

I can see you too, sitting there!

That's the proof. If you said you *hadn't* seen me, it'd prove what people keep saying, about me not interacting properly with the world around me. You'd only exist in my mind. But you know you don't. Because if you did, I could snuff you out. Like putting out the ostrich. Or is it tiger? Then you'd disappear too.

Just like—that!

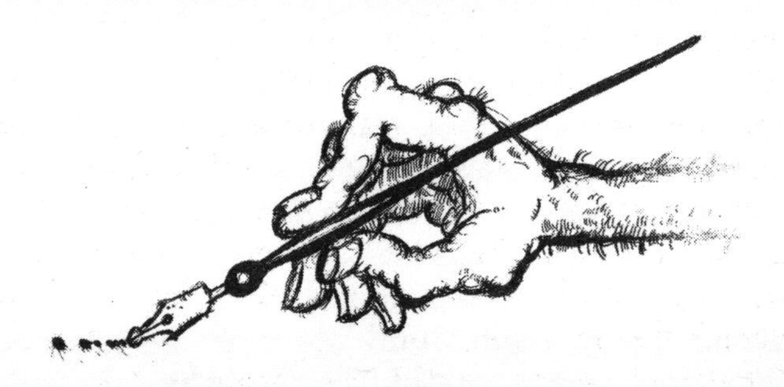

The Happy Alien

JEAN URE

Last summer, a very strange thing happened to my gran. She woke up to find a bus ticket on her table.

This may not sound very strange to you, but trust me! It was strange.

My gran is what Mum calls eccentric. What me and Ria (Ria's my sister) call *loopy*. I mean, we love her to bits, but she is seriously out of this world. She has these obsessions. Her main obsession is clutter.

'Everything in its place,' she says. Meaning: we do not leave clothes draped over the backs of chairs, we do not dump stuff in the middle of the floor, and we certainly do not pile junk half a metre high on the tops of tables. She'd freak if she saw my bedroom! Gran's flat always looks like a giant vacuum cleaner has just breezed through it. Every surface clean and clear. *Free of clutter*. What I'm saying is, when Gran went to bed that night, the night I'm talking about, you can take it from me: *there was no bus ticket on her table*.

But there it was, in the morning. She rang up Mum in a right state, claiming that Her Next Door had somehow managed to get into the flat while she was sleeping. Mum didn't ask her how. All sense flies out of the window when Gran gets on to the subject of Her Next Door. Her Next Door was another of her obsessions. Gran was convinced she'd got it in for her. Now she was muttering darkly about the Evil Eye. The bus ticket, she said, was A Sign.

'Don't worry,' said Mum. 'I'll send the kids round. They'll soon sort things out.' She beamed brightly at me and Ria. 'You don't mind going round to Gran's, do you?'

'S'ppose not,' said Ria.

'Aaron?'

Well, it was holiday time; what could I say?

'I'd go myself,' said Mum, 'but I've absolutely got to get this work finished.'

We didn't really mind. Gran's totally off the wall, but she is kind of fun. She makes me laugh! I did warn Ria, though, that we'd got to take it seriously. Ria has this tendency to be a bit frivolous. A bit *flip*. You can't treat Gran like that.

'OK!' I said, as Gran slid back the bolts on the front door. (She's got four of them, plus a normal lock, plus a chain, plus a spy hole.) 'Show us the scene of the crime!'

Gran was pretty pleased that we were being so professional about it. She's more used to being told, 'You're just imagining things.' She led us through to the sitting room.

'There!' she said. 'I've left everything just as I found it.'

The table was over by the window, and it was bare except for a vase of dried flowers (neatly standing on a mat) and this little screwed up ball of paper.

'Undo that,' I said to Ria.

'It's a bus ticket,' said Ria. 'And a bit of silver foil . . . ooh! It's off an *egg*.'

She meant one of those miniature Easter eggs full of cream. Personally I think they're disgusting, but she goes for them big time.

'Never mind the egg,' I said. 'What about the bus ticket?'

'Says route 170,' said Ria.

'Where's that go?'

Ria peered closer. 'Says, *valid from Stage 1, valid to Stage 46*.'

Hm! None the wiser.

'It's Her Next Door,' said Gran. 'Look what she's done to my flowers!'

A couple of the flowers, a bright red one and a bright yellow one, had been taken out of the vase and laid on the table. Both the heads had been pulled off. It did seem a bit ominous.

'It's a sign,' said Gran. 'You mark my words!'

It was certainly a mystery. I was intrigued! I'm very interested in this kind of thing. Solving puzzles, finding rational explanations. This one was quite a challenge. For starters, Gran's flat is on the third floor, and I just didn't see how anyone could have got up there. There's a fire escape at the *back*, but Gran's sitting room is at the front. The wall outside is bare brick. No trees, no drain pipes: nothing.

'She's putting the Evil Eye,' said Gran.

'But Gran,' I said, 'how could she have got in?'

Gran looked at me as if I were daft. 'Through the window, of course!'

Me and Ria both turned, to gaze at the window. Gran is so security conscious that she has mesh across it—except for just a tiny slit right at the top, which she leaves open in hot weather. She also leaves the light on, all day and all night, 'just to make sure'. It's another of her obsessions.

'What's her name?' said Ria. 'Her Next Door?'

'You may well ask,' said Gran.

'I am asking,' said Ria. 'Could be important!'

Gran sniffed. 'It's *Smith*—or so she says.'

'Hm.' Ria nodded. 'Obviously an alias.'

'Well, I could have told you that,' said Gran.

I listened to this zany exchange in growing amazement. What on earth had the woman's name got to do with anything? And why should it be an alias?

'Don't you see?' cried Ria. 'She's an alien in disguise! She's probably—' she dropped her voice—'a *shape shifter*.'

Well, Gran latched on to that idea immediately. That really got her going. A shape shifter! An alien shape shifter! Shape shifting through windows at dead of night to pull the heads off dried flowers and leave bus tickets on the table.

'Are you mad?' I hissed at Ria.

She giggled. 'Well, think of some other explanation!'

I couldn't; not offhand. But unlike Ria, who is totally uncontrolled when it comes to imagination, I firmly believe that there is always a rational explanation if you only look hard enough. I don't buy into all this supernatural stuff. And I *certainly* don't buy into shape shifters.

We spent the rest of the morning searching for rational explanations. First off I made Ria stand on a chair and try stuffing herself through the window, just to prove to my satisfaction that it couldn't be done. Next I went outside to conduct ballistic tests, seeing if I could lob pebbles or sticks through the window; but that couldn't be done, either. Even if it could have been, I didn't quite see where it would have got us, except that I do believe in being thorough. You have to eliminate all possibilities.

Gran, meanwhile, was busy ringing Mum to tell her about the shape shifter. Mum then spoke to me and said, 'Aaron, can you *please* stop your sister putting these ideas into your gran's head?' At least she knew it was Ria, and not me. But something plainly had to be done. Gran was in a lather, Mum was going spare . . . there had got to be a rational explanation!

'Let's be logical,' I said. 'Let's find out about the bus.'

So off we went to the bus station, and spoke to an inspector. We showed him the ticket—which I saw was dated just over a week ago—and he was really helpful. He obviously understood that we were conducting a serious investigation; we weren't just a couple of kids messing about. He told us that bus no. 170 ran from the other side of town. Stage 46 was Reeves Corner, and Stage 1, where it had come from, was Tipsy Hill, which was in a place called Tiddenham. Well! It seemed obvious to me what we had to do next: go to Tiddenham.

Ria wanted to know what for. I said, 'To check it out, of course!' She may have a vivid imagination, my sister, but she is totally lacking in any sort of logical thought process.

We went back to Gran's to assure her that we were on the case, and to ring Mum and tell her what we were up to. Mum said, 'I know Tiddenham! It's *tiddly*. It's just a village!'

'All the better,' I said.

'Well, so long as you're back by tea time,' said Mum. She's always pretty relaxed. She doesn't believe in molly coddling. 'Just solve the mystery and set your gran's mind at rest!'

Mum has total faith in me. I'm not sure that Ria does, but when it comes to action she does what I tell her. Right now I was telling her to 'Move it!' We didn't have all day.

On our way out of the flats we actually bumped into . . . Her Next Door!

'The alien!' whispered Ria.

She didn't look like an alien, she looked like a sweet old lady. Of course I knew what my sister would say: she would say that only went to show how cunning she was.

'It's what shape shifters *do*!'

My sister watches too much *Star Trek*.

The sweet old lady toddled up to us, beaming. She had a postcard in her hand.

'I wonder,' she goes, in this sweet old lady voice, 'if you would be very kind and put this in the box for me? Save my poor legs.'

We practically snatched it from her and ran. Not that I believed in any of this shape shifter stuff. Not for a minute! But it's kind of dark, in the hallway of Gran's flats. Plus I couldn't help wondering whether that sweet old lady wasn't just a little bit *too* sweet . . .

The minute we got outside, Ria was agitating to know what the postcard said.

'Who's it to? Read it, read it!'

I hesitated for just a second, on account of having this feeling that other people's mail might be private, and in that second Ria rudely snatched it from me. She has no scruples whatsoever. She probably doesn't even know what scruples are.

'So, all right,' I said. 'What's it say?'

Ria pulled a face. 'Dear-Madge-I-did-enjoy-your-visit-last-week. Next-time,' gabbled Ria, 'I-will-come-to-you. So-relieved-about-Maggie. I-would-have-felt-dreadfully-guilty-if-anything-had-happened-to-her. Much-love-Sylvia.'

'Well, that tells us a lot,' I said.

'Obviously written in code,' said Ria. 'Sylvia Smith . . . it's got to be an alias! Nobody's called Sylvia Smith.'

Actually I would have thought that quite a lot of people were, but before I could point this out to her Ria was reading the address and her eyes were popping out on stalks. 'Hey! Get this! It's addressed to someone in Tiddenham!'

'What?' I grabbed the card back from her. And there it was, plain as day: Mrs Madge Henshaw, Tipsy Cottage, Tipsy Hill, Tiddenham. We were on to something! The question was, what?

'The plot thickens,' said Ria.

I said, 'What plot?' Hoping that she might be going to say something helpful. Something intelligent. Instead she gave this mad cackle.

'Alien plot to take over the earth!'

'Look, just stop with the smart mouth,' I said. I was beginning to wonder if maybe Gran wasn't as dotty as we all thought she was. Maybe Her Next Door really did have it in for her.

I said this to Ria, but all she said was, '*Shape shifter!*'

I had to admit we were no nearer solving the central mystery of how anyone, and especially a sweet old lady, could have managed to get through Gran's window and into the flat; but at least we now had a link between the sweet old lady and the bus ticket.

At this point I am going to throw in a cryptic observation: remember the silver paper! That is all I shall say. *Bear it in mind.*

And now to continue. Little did she know it, but Her Next Door had played right into our hands. She had been too clever by half! If she was the guilty party, that is. I still couldn't make up my mind. All I knew was that she had to be involved somehow. This was our lucky break! It gave us the very opportunity we needed. Instead of putting the card in the box, we would take it with us and deliver it in person to Mrs Madge Henshaw.

'Good idea,' said Ria. 'Go and suss her out . . . I'll know at once,' she said, 'if she's a shape shifter!'

We got off the bus at Stage 1, just like on the ticket, and an old man sitting on a seat in the sunshine told us how to get to Tipsy Cottage.

'Have you noticed?' hissed Ria, as we set off up the hill. 'Everyone's *old*.'

'So what?' I said.

'They're all aliens!' said Ria.

Sometimes I think my sister takes after Gran. She is *very* obsessive. So am I, in my own more logical way. I will stop at nothing to find rational explanations! I just knew there had to be one. I'd had enough of all this alien rubbish!

All the same, I did get a few uneasy prickles down my spine when we finally fetched up at Tipsy Cottage and saw it crouched there, low and squat and spooky, half hidden behind a giant yew tree, all by itself at the far end of the lane. Suddenly I wasn't sure that what we were doing was sensible. Even Ria had stopped her stupid jokes.

'Maybe we ought to g-go to the p-police?' she quavered.

'And say what? Shape shifters have been crawling through Gran's window? Aliens are taking over the earth?'

'Oh, don't be *stupid*!' said Ria. 'Just tell them what happened!'

'Please, officer, someone left a bus ticket on my Gran's table . . . I don't think so!'

'So what are we going to *do*?'

'You stay here,' I said. 'If I'm not back in five minutes—'

'Don't leave me!' shrieked Ria.

So we went up the path together, and knocked on the door, and this little old lady came to open it. *Another* little old lady. Yeah? I didn't dare to look at Ria.

'We . . . um . . . happened to be . . . um . . . passing,' I stammered, 'so we . . . ah . . . thought we'd . . . ah . . . give you this.'

I thrust the postcard at her.

'From Sylvia!' said the old lady. 'How very kind! Do come in, the pair of you.'

I said, 'Er—' Ria was already backing away, down the path. I was about to back after her, when the old lady gave a sudden cry.

'Why, here's Maggie come to see you!'

Maggie. Take a pause, because that is a clue.

Have you guessed? Maggie the magpie . . . strutting up the hall with something in her beak. Something bright and shiny . . . a ball of silver paper!

I don't think Ria got it even then. Her head was too full of aliens. But I did! I got it. It all fell into place . . . the rational explanation.

I checked with the old lady, to make sure, but it was just as I thought. She told us how she'd taken Maggie with her, to stay with her old friend Sylvia Smith. Her Next Door. How Her Next Door, not being used to having magpies about the place, had left the window open—and Maggie had flown off.

'My dear,' said the old lady, 'I was almost beside myself! I thought she was gone forever. But there she was, the darling, waiting for me next morning!'

We pieced together what must have happened. Maggie had taken the screwed-up ball of bus ticket and silver paper out of the bin and made her exit through the window. She had then been lured by the light in Gran's room, hopped through the gap, dumped the bus ticket on the table and helped herself to a couple of flowers. Quite logical behaviour—for a magpie.

'So there you are,' I said to Ria, as we sat on the bus going home. 'Nothing whatsoever to do with shape shifters.'

'Well, but it could have been,' said Ria.

'Well, but it *wasn't*. I told you there had to be a rational explanation.'

'Don't think it's as interesting as shape shifters,' said Ria.

It is strange how different we are. I actually prefer rational explanations. I find them more satisfying. Gran obviously does, too.

'I knew it was Her Next Door!' she said. 'I knew it all along!'

She was so chuffed at being right for once, and not having everyone accuse her of imagining things, that she actually went and told Her Next Door all about it, and now, guess what? They're best mates!

Ria says what's happened is that Her Next Door has turned Gran into a fellow alien, but Mum says that's OK.

'So long as she's a *happy* alien, that's all that matters!'

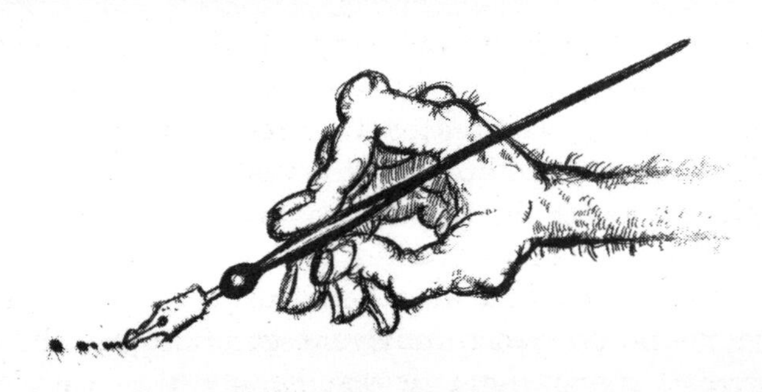

The Drowning

MALCOLM ROSE

An uncanny hush had fallen on Lower Halfway. The only people left were six police officers who were combing the village to make sure it was deserted. Some of the inhabitants had left willingly, setting up homes on higher ground in Halfway itself. Some had been forced from their houses by the water company's heartless bailiffs. Now abandoned, the condemned village looked immensely sad and unwanted.

A young policeman closed the door of 13 Carr Lane, hesitated for a few seconds and took a deep breath. Making up his mind, he reported into his walkie-talkie, 'Leo here. Carr Lane checked, all houses clear.'

A crackly voice replied, 'OK. You're the last. Perimeter fence secure. Time to get out. We're closing the dam gates.'

'Roger.'

Leo took one last look down the road towards the church. It was strange to think that an entire community could vanish just like that. No longer would he cycle down the lane, call in at the pub, and make secret visits to Katie. In a matter of days, the valley would be one huge lake. Lower Halfway would be silenced forever and erased from the map. To protect Katie from harm, Leo was satisfied that more than a village was being erased. No matter what, Leo would always protect his beloved Katie.

The church spire was the first part of Lower Halfway to appear above the still water, like the mast of a shipwreck. A few rainless days later, the whole of the roof emerged. No one had seen the village's chapel for thirty years, since the valley had been flooded to make a new reservoir, but in the long dry summer the process had gone into reverse. The water level was dropping day-by-day. The pub's chimney was next to poke into the air, followed by the ridge of the village school. Then the roofs of several homes broke the surface all together as if an out-going tide had exposed a sunken armada. Drought was resurrecting Lower Halfway.

'Weird,' Ricky said from behind the wire fencing. 'It's like watching someone build a place from the top downwards.'

The boy standing next to Ricky Muir had his fingers entwined in the diamond shaped webbing. 'My dad's got wire cutters.'

'So?'

Mike made scissors of two fingers. 'Snip, snip, snip. We're in.'

The four boys looked up at the sign, *OUT OF BOUNDS*, and the bundle of razor wire four metres up. At the same time, they all said, 'Yeah.'

By the time that Mike had cut through the fencing, behind a bush where the gap would not be noticed, most of Lower Halfway had resurfaced. Like archaeologists who had just discovered a lost city, Ricky and his friends could not resist the temptation to explore. The secluded valley was hidden from Halfway so no one was going to see the four lads scrambling down the bank at twilight and walking along the old cracked road into the ghost village.

It was like wandering back through time.

Mike lifted the browned metallic skeleton of an ancient bike from a puddle and then dropped it again. 'Don't make them like that any more.'

Outside the village store, Ricky bent down, picked a worn old penny out of the dried sludge and showed it to the others. 'Funny money.'

'Could be valuable, that,' said Mohammed.

Ricky slipped it into his pocket.

The telephone box was amazing. Thirty years before, rising water had pushed against the door, sealing it, making it a permanent bubble in the lake, the opposite of a goldfish bowl. The telephone itself was a strange contraption with all sorts of unfamiliar pushbuttons. Danny lifted the heavy receiver. 'Hello? Anybody there? This is the next century calling.'

'Look.' Mohammed flicked through the pages of the directory, still dry in the waterproof time capsule.

'More fun over there,' Mike said, pointing through the thick glass at the cemetery.

The church had been the heart of Lower Halfway for seven hundred years. One of the last sounds in the now silent village had been the gloomy clang of the church bells, signalling the doom of the entire valley. The boys made straight for the graveyard where generations of former villagers still lay. Some headstones had keeled over in the mud but they were intact and the carving was still clear.

Talking to Ricky, Danny said, 'Your lot used to live in Lower Halfway, didn't they? Your ancestors'll be buried here.'

They soon found gravestones for four Muirs who had died between 1890 and 1961. Looking at them, Ricky wondered about the grandad he'd never seen. Cliff Muir had walked out on his wife and his son, called Tranmere, before the flood. He was probably alive and well somewhere but, even if he was dead, his body couldn't have been brought back to his home village.

In the middle of the cemetery, Mike spun round and called cheerfully to the others, 'Bet they was right mad at the flood. Swimmin' in their graves.'

Ricky was about to step inside the church itself, an empty shell deserted by both God and its congregation, when Mohammed shivered and said, 'Let's go.'

Realizing that Mohammed was uneasy about going into the creepy abandoned church, Ricky agreed. 'All right.'

Relics were scattered down Carr Lane: broken crockery, abandoned toys, an unwanted pram. Each piece had a hidden history and, like the headstones, represented a life lost to Lower Halfway. The boys slipped into a house that had been stripped. There was no carpet and no furniture. The walls were bare brick and the concrete floor was covered with the mushy remains of wallpaper and plaster that had cascaded from the saturated brickwork. In the kitchen, Mike had to turn on his torch. The spotlight picked out a tiled floor, an empty pantry, a huge sink, cupboards, and two rotten doors. One led to the back yard, the other was internal.

'Seen enough?' Mohammed asked anxiously.

'Not quite.'

Guided by the beam, Ricky and Mike headed for the internal door. It came away in Ricky's hands—half opening, half collapsing—to reveal stone steps going down into total darkness. A terrible stench drifted upwards. 'A cellar!' Mike cried. 'Great. Down we go.'

'Do you think we should?' asked Danny.

'Course.'

'It stinks,' Mohammed muttered.

Mohammed and Danny exchanged a glance. Even in the darkness, they could each see that the other was scared. They couldn't walk away, though, because that would have made them cowards. They tiptoed down the gritty steps into the cellar close behind the other two.

There was no light at all except for Mike's torch. The cellar was a disgusting swimming pool and the stagnant water looked filthy like oil. Leading the way, Mike stopped on the lowest dry step and scanned the spotlight slowly round the walls. There was a disused electricity meter, the top of a decrepit work-bench, empty shelves, and a water pipe.

All four of them leapt and gasped at the same time. The narrow beam had found a human skeleton, its ribs, neck, and skull poking out of the water. Straightaway, the boys turned round and rushed back up the steps, through the kitchen and out into the fresh air.

Ricky's grandma had always been a bit odd. Half the time she seemed to be in a world of her own. As the hot summer stretched out, her sanity seemed to dwindle along with the water level.

Ricky asked her about Lower Halfway but it was Leo—the man he called Grandad—who responded.

'Why are you asking?'

Ricky knew he shouldn't have gone to the old village so he couldn't tell them what he'd seen and done. He couldn't tell them that, every time he closed his eyes, he saw that dreadful skeleton. He shrugged. 'Just because you can see it, I suppose.'

Grandma snapped into life. 'Never to go there, love.'

'You can't,' he replied. 'It's fenced off.'

'That's because it's dangerous,' his grandad said.

In her faraway voice, Grandma added, 'Dangerous and evil.'

Quickly, Leo injected some common sense. 'Those old buildings could collapse any time and it's against the law to trespass.'

'Yeah, but isn't it strange to see your old place come to life again?' asked Ricky. 'Wouldn't you want to go back and take a look—if it was safe?'

Grandma shook her head. 'It was never that great, love.' Then she stared out of the window.

'How's your grandma?' Ricky's dad asked.

'Oh, you know.'

'That bad, eh?' Tranmere sighed. 'I guess this weather's tiring her out.'

'You grew up in Lower Halfway, didn't you?' asked Ricky.

'Hardly,' Tranmere answered. 'I was a baby when they flooded the valley.'

'So, you don't remember your dad—my real grandad—either.'

'Leo's the only dad I ever had. Your grandma never wanted to talk about it—not surprisingly. The only thing I know about my real dad is, he was called Cliff. Oh, and I know to my cost which football team he supported.'

With a grin, Ricky said, 'Tranmere Rovers.'
'Yeah, right.'

Down on all fours, Ricky scrambled through the hole behind the hedge and, torch in hand, made his way towards the drowned village as night fell. It was much more frightening to explore on his own but this time it was personal. He thought he'd worked out a way of discovering more about Cliff Muir and he was determined to see it through.

In the old telephone box, Ricky thumbed through the 1970 directory by torchlight until he found an address for C. P. Muir: 9 Carr Lane, Lower Halfway. Now, Ricky just had to find the house and hope that something remained inside, some clue about his grandad. He also hoped to steer clear of the house with the skeleton in the cellar.

Walking along Carr Lane, Ricky was brought to a halt by the sound of scrabbling claws on his left. 'Rats,' he told himself with a shudder. He wasn't the only one scavenging in the ruins. The shattering shriek and sudden swoop of a hunting owl sent the rats scampering for safety. Jolted, Ricky hurried up, shining his light on the succession of front doors. He'd feel safer inside his grandparent's home.

Yet, when he found number 9, its rotten front door open, Ricky groaned aloud, feeling sick in his stomach. This was the house he'd entered with Mike, Mohammed, and Danny. Suddenly, being indoors had lost its appeal. The warmth of day had not yet melted away but, for the first time this summer, Ricky felt cold. Why was there a skeleton in his grandma's old house?

Determined not to abandon his search for information, Ricky made for the upstairs rooms, keeping well clear of the cellar. As soon as he focused his light on the staircase, though, he realized that he would not be able to get up. The wooden steps had decomposed and wouldn't hold his weight. Instead, he cast the spotlight around the downstairs rooms again, looking for morsels in the sludge.

In what had once been a sitting room, the torchlight picked out some glass by the crumbling fireplace. Ricky bent down and wiped away the filth. It was a picture frame and behind it, protected from water, was a photograph of a woman and a man who was uncannily similar to his dad. He had a wide grin and she seemed to be forcing a smile. Putting the torch down, Ricky carefully extracted the fragile photo and turned it over. Four scrawled words looked as if they had been written in ink on wet blotting paper. Even so, he could make out a faint *Cliff and Katie 1969*. Holding the picture was the nearest he'd ever been to his real grandad. He smiled, slipped the photo into a pocket and continued to rummage around.

His head began to ache. The stink, the torchlight, and the tension were getting to him. The kitchen cupboards held nothing at all. When he stood upright, he felt dizzy and he found himself staring at the doorway to that awful cellar. Despite wanting to go home, he was drawn to the stone steps. He shone the light down and guessed that the water had retreated further. He shook his heavy head, trying to resist the impulse to go down. But, he told himself, some new clue might have emerged by now. Gingerly, he put a foot on the first step. Unable to stop himself, he descended slowly, unwillingly, as if he were going into a dungeon or torture chamber.

The skeleton was propped against the far wall in a sitting position. Its leg bones were bulges in the mud.

Fighting the urge to run away, Ricky played the light over it. It was big enough to be an adult. No doubt it had been stripped of its flesh by the patient work of fish. Ricky was standing in the middle of the room, his trainers squelching in the mire, his feet damp. Tearing his eyes away from the remains, he turned right around checking every surface for anything interesting. He saw nothing until he completed the circle and got back to the skeleton. It was then that he noticed that the bony wrists were manacled to the water pipe.

The spotlight lingered on the handcuffs while Ricky registered that he was looking at a murder. Someone had chained the victim in the cellar before the village had been flooded. His spine tingling with shock, Ricky gulped down tainted air. He was imagining how it must have felt if this person had been conscious as the water came pouring down the cellar steps, covering waist, chest, and neck. Helpless against the handcuffs, surely the victim would have screamed and screamed. The cellar was a torture chamber after all.

Ricky let out a yelp when he heard the sound of footfalls on the steps and a light behind him. He spun round and his torch picked out a policeman's uniform.

'Ricky!'

It was his grandad.

'What are you doing here? I told you to keep out!'

While Ricky shone a light towards his grandad's face, Leo glanced towards the skeleton. How, Ricky asked himself, did he know exactly where to look? 'I was just . . . doing a bit of research,' he stuttered. 'Family history and all that.'

Leo shook his head in irritation. 'And what do you think you've found here?'

By the light of his torch, Ricky gazed into Leo's face and realized what had happened all those years ago.

He also understood why his grandma was so detached. 'This is my real grandad, isn't it? Cliff.'

Leo took a deep breath. 'If you must know, Cliff Muir was a drunken bully who used to beat your grandma.'

Trying to be brave, Ricky said, 'So you killed him.' His voice came out quaky.

'One day, when she couldn't take it any more and he was completely drunk, she lured him down here and . . .' He nodded towards the skeleton.

'No,' Ricky cried. 'You can't just blame Grandma. She wouldn't have handcuffs.' He looked accusingly at Leo. 'You did it together.'

'Understand this, Ricky. I'll do anything to protect Katie. Anything.'

'That's why you're here, isn't it? You've come to get rid of the evidence—the skeleton you thought no one would ever see!'

'You were always too clever for your own good. I won't have her accused of murder. It'd destroy her.'

'So, what are you going to do?'

Leo paused before muttering darkly, 'You've made it very awkward. I can't trust you to keep quiet.'

'He was my grandad.'

Leo pulled a set of handcuffs from his belt. 'What the water's done once, it can do again.' He grabbed Ricky and slapped him down roughly in the silt. 'I won't let you ruin things.'

Ricky could not escape. Leo was a big man, much more powerful than Ricky, and he'd arrested hundreds of people this way. The only thing Ricky could do was shout and scream.

'We gagged Cliff. The bandage has decayed—like his clothes. Now, I'm going to do the same to you, though no one will hear you anyway.'

Ricky cried, 'The place won't flood any more.'

'Don't you believe it. This hot spell will end and Lower Halfway'll go under all over again.'

Before he knew it, Ricky was manacled to the pipe and silenced like his grandad had been thirty years before. Ricky could only watch as Leo kicked at the skeleton, grinding the softened bone beneath his big boots. Leo's face was a mixture of hatred and madness.

When he'd finished, Leo took up his torch again and went to leave but hesitated. 'I'm sorry it had to turn out like this,' he said, 'but it's your own fault. You should've done what you were told and kept away.' Then he dashed up the steps towards fresh air, leaving Ricky to wait for rain.

It was after midnight. A desperate Tranmere sat with Ricky's mum who had her fingers entangled in her hair and tears streaming down her face. Leo was kneeling by Katie, squeezing her hand supportively. 'I'm sorry it had to be me,' he was saying, 'but when the message came into the station . . . Well, I recognized Ricky's description. He was seen playing about by this car just before it went up in flames. The forensic people are there now but . . . the fire was very fierce, I'm afraid. They're not sure they're going to find anything.'

'It couldn't have been Ricky!' his mum cried.

Softly, Leo said, 'But we have to face up to the fact that he's missing. He's never been this late before, has he?'

Tranmere shook his head.

'I still don't believe it! It wasn't Ricky.'

In their grief, none of them saw the door swing open. They heard only a weak voice. 'No, it wasn't me.'

'Ricky!' His mum was the first to get to him and take him in her arms. 'We've been so worried. What happened? Look at you. You're in a terrible state!'

Ricky's clothes and face were stained with mud, his hair was matted, and his mouth swollen, his bruised wrists were shackled together, and he stank. In the moment before his eyes closed and he collapsed with exhaustion, he looked at Leo and said, 'The pipe's been under water for ages. It's not as strong as it used to be.'

Katie stared in horror at Leo with her mouth open but no words came out. She had been haunted for years by their ugly crime but now, like Lower Halfway itself, their secret was hidden no longer.

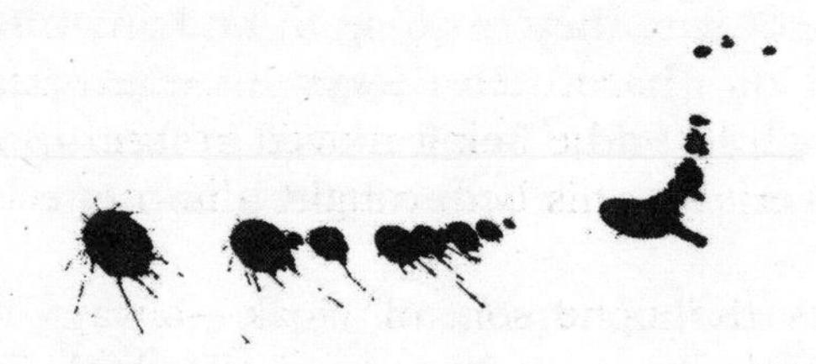

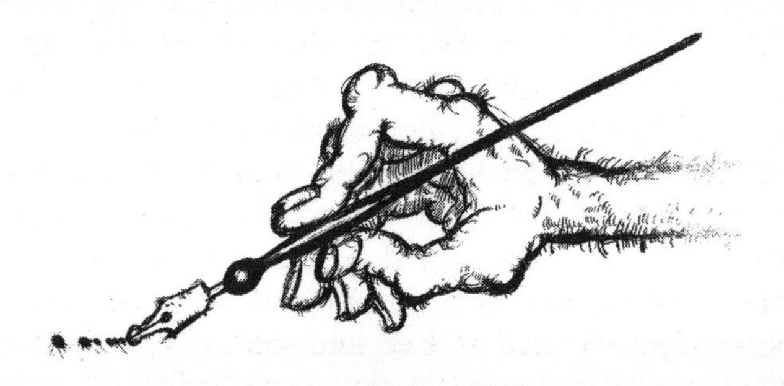

Bad Dreams

DOUGLAS HILL

Tim came awake knowing that if he opened his eyes he would see something that would make him scream in terror.

Even so, slowly, unwillingly, his eyelids parted.

As always, it was the middle of the night, with a dim light from the hall reaching into his bedroom. As always, he felt wide awake.

But he was sure he was dreaming. It *had* to be a dream. The monstrosity in his room had to be from the depths of nightmare. It *couldn't* be real.

Like all the others, before, it wore a hooded cloak reaching to the floor. Also as with the others, the cloak parted slightly as the being moved around the room. So Tim, cowering in his bed, caught glimpses of its hidden form.

Always the same sort of cloak—always a different horror inside.

This one had a ghastly skull-face, with huge eyes bulging from the sockets and long saw-teeth that glittered wetly as it lurched towards Tim.

But as Tim cried out in panic, the monster grew blurred. In another instant it vanished—just as Tim's mother rushed in, switching on the light.

'Timmy!' She gathered him into a hug. 'Another bad dream?'

Tim nodded. 'Like the others—a horrible thing coming at me . . . '

'Never mind,' his mother soothed. 'It's gone now.'

'But why does it keep happening?' Tim asked unhappily.

'I don't know,' his mother said. 'Maybe it'll stop just as suddenly as it started. And remember—they're just dreams. They're not *real.*'

Tim wanted to believe her. But ever since the nightmares started, they always *seemed* real. They weren't crazy and mixed-up like ordinary dreams. And the memory of them didn't fade, the way ordinary dreams did.

So, next morning, the dream of the skull-monster still felt real, even in daylight. But at least he would have one or two nights, now, of unbroken sleep. That was how it happened—the same kind of nightmare, every two or three days.

Heading for the kitchen, for breakfast, he heard his parents talking—about him.

'Maybe it's because we moved house,' his father was saying. 'That's a big shake-up for a boy of eleven, leaving the first home he ever had.'

'But we've been here two months,' his mother said. 'And the dreams only started two *weeks* ago.' She sighed. 'I think it's all that spooky horror stuff he's always reading or watching on TV . . . '

His father chuckled. 'All the kids like that stuff. He'll probably just grow out of it, dreams and all, before long.'

'But it's affecting him *now*,' his mother insisted. 'He's losing sleep, looking pale . . . We ought to take him to the doctor.'

'I'm not sick,' Tim said, going in to join them. 'I don't need a doctor.'

'Maybe you need a witch-doctor,' his father grinned.

'We need someone who knows about dreams and things, Timmy,' his mother said firmly. 'And who doesn't make jokes about it.'

His father laughed. 'Anyway, if the house is haunted, it should've been cheaper.'

But Tim didn't smile. He was sure that their new house *was* haunted, in a way.

Certainly he knew that his problem had nothing to do with moving, or with the books and TV he liked. Something else was causing his bad dreams. They had begun soon after his father had noticed a shallow dent, high on one wall in Tim's room. His father had chopped out the plaster at that spot—and found something buried in it.

A small flat tablet, like baked clay, with a ribbon of thin metal wound around it. It looked old, for the tablet was chipped and the metal was tarnished. And it had strange markings all over its surfaces.

'I wonder how that got in there?' Tim's father had said.

'Maybe it's a magic amulet,' Tim had said. Amulets with special powers often appeared in the stories he liked.

His father had laughed. 'Then you have it, Tim,' he said. 'You're the magic expert.'

Tim had taken the object, but he hadn't really wanted it. Somehow it made him uneasy—mostly because it had been *hidden* in his wall. In the stories, amulets that were hidden were always uncanny, and usually evil.

So he had decided to get rid of it. And since in many stories it could be dangerous to try to destroy an evil amulet, he simply threw it into the rubbish, which was collected that day.

It had all seemed easy, and Tim had felt relieved. But the next night he had his first terror-dream, a cloaked monstrosity gibbering and swirling around his room, red eyes flaring within the cloak's folds.

And it kept happening—more nightmare monsters in cloaks, invading his room. Tim thought they might be some sort of ghosts, since he knew ghosts often did the same repeated actions, over and over. But, ghosts or demons, he had no doubt at all that they were haunting him because of the amulet.

It was just like one of his comics—where the Shadow-Master, enemy of demonic forces, battled a nameless evil that had been awakened by an ancient amulet. In the same way, he thought, taking the amulet from the wall had stirred up something evil, to invade his dreams.

Of course no one would believe that. They'd be like his father, not taking his nightmares seriously. Or like his mother, who thought that doctors would help—and who had in fact made an appointment with their family doctor.

But Tim was miserably sure that there wasn't much that doctors—or anyone—could do about his dreams.

The night before the appointment with the doctor, Tim again woke into terror. A cloaked monster, a towering giant, stamped around the room, growling, its cloak showing glimpses of matted fur and glinting tusks. But as always, when he cried out as it loomed over him, it faded and vanished. And when his mother arrived, she was hopeful as well as comforting.

'Don't worry,' she said. 'I'm sure the doctor will help.'

But, as Tim expected, when they saw the doctor he didn't help at all.

He had a cluttered desk and a full waiting room, and he clearly thought that worrying about dreams was wasting his time. He barely listened to Tim's mother, barely looked at Tim—then muttered something about nightmares being normal in 'imaginative children', and offered a prescription for a tonic.

Still, Tim's mother persisted—so the doctor grumpily agreed to send Tim to an expert on children's ailments, at the local hospital. But the expert, when they saw him, proved to be very self-important but quite useless. After asking Tim a few questions he 'saw the problem'. Tim, he said, was reading and watching too much 'supernatural rubbish'. If he stopped doing so, the expert said, the nightmares would stop.

Tim tried to say that he had been reading and watching such things for ages, without having nightmares. But the expert had made his mind up, and didn't listen.

'What a waste of time!' Tim's mother fumed, on the way home.

'I don't think doctors know much about dreams,' Tim murmured.

That night, Tim had another bad dream—with a lumpy-skinned monster *slithering* around the room on whatever it had for feet. Then, in the morning after that dream, while Tim was yawning glumly over his breakfast, the phone rang. When his mother came back from answering it, she looked both doubtful and hopeful at the same time.

'That was strange,' she said. 'A woman with an odd name—Lethe Linn—some kind of doctor and psychiatrist. She saw the hospital notes about Timmy's dreams, and wants to come and see him.'

'A doctor, doing a home visit?' Tim's father smiled. 'Now that *is* strange.'

'She might help,' his mother said, then turned to Tim. 'A psychiatrist is a doctor who deals with the mind . . . '

'I *know*,' Tim muttered. 'And I'm not crazy.'

'Of course not!' his mother gasped. 'But dreams happen in the mind, so maybe that's the kind of doctor we need.'

'She can't be any more useless than that *expert*,' Tim's father said.

'Right,' his mother said. 'She gave me her number, so I'll ring her back.'

'Lethe Linn, was it?' his father asked. 'Sounds foreign. All the best head-doctors are foreign.'

So Tim's mother rang back, and the mysterious doctor agreed to come around that very evening.

Tim wasn't hopeful at all. But he did feel curious, that evening, when the doorbell rang.

And Doctor Lethe Linn was definitely unusual.

She was small, no taller than Tim, slim and graceful in a long green dress. She was also quite pretty—though she was wearing a great deal of thick make-up—with huge luminous eyes under a tousle of black hair, and a sweet smile. And she did seem foreign, with a noticeable accent.

Tim liked her at once. Especially when she told him to call her Lethe, then settled herself on the couch beside him, fixed her amazing eyes on him, and smiled.

'Now,' she said, 'tell me all about these bad dreams.'

Tim began hesitantly. But Lethe listened intently,

her gaze never shifting. So Tim relaxed and spoke more freely, describing every nightmare monster in detail.

'They're all so alike . . . ' Tim's father began. But Lethe held up a hand.

'Please,' she said. 'Tim is speaking for himself very well—and I need to hear these things from *him*, only.'

Tim smiled to himself as his parents sat back in obedient silence. And Lethe began quietly asking a few questions—what the monsters seemed to be doing, whether they were really threatening him. And still she listened closely to his every word, never once looking as if she thought that what he was saying was boring or childish or a waste of her time.

'Tell me now, Tim,' she said at last, 'what you think may be making this happen.'

'It's . . . ' Tim began, and then stopped himself. Under Lethe's attentive gaze he had almost blurted out his belief that an evil amulet had caused it. But she'd think that was silly, he felt, and might lose interest. And he didn't want that to happen.

'It's . . . er . . . a mystery,' he went on lamely. 'Mum thinks it's the books and TV that I like . . . '

Lethe smiled. 'Tell me about them.'

So Tim told her about his favourite comics, like the Shadow-Master—and about the series of scary books, the *Chill Factor*, that he collected—and about his best TV programmes, the eerie *Spook City* and of course *Bexy the Demon Hunter*.

'And you have liked these things,' Lethe said, 'for some time?'

'For ages,' Tim said.

'And yet your strange dreams began only a short while ago?' Lethe said.

'Right,' Tim agreed.

Lethe nodded thoughtfully, then turned to his

parents. 'Would you leave us for a short time?' she asked. 'There may be things that would be better said in private . . . '

Tim's mother frowned. 'Timmy doesn't have secrets from us . . . '

'How would we know, if they're secrets?' his father laughed. 'Come on, love.'

When they were alone, Lethe smiled gently at Tim. 'There was something you started to say, then changed your mind. Why was that?'

Tim flushed. 'Because you'd think I'm a silly kid . . . ' he mumbled.

'No, I would not,' she said. 'I take you very seriously indeed. And I must know as much as I can about you. Please—tell me what you were going to say.'

So, with some embarrassment, Tim told her about the amulet found in his wall, which he had thrown away. 'Maybe moving it,' he said, 'let the evil out.'

'So,' Lethe said slowly. 'That is how it happened.'

Tim peered at her. 'Do you *believe* it was magic?'

Lethe got suddenly to her feet. 'I believe,' she said, 'that you are a very pleasant and perfectly normal boy—and that your bad dreams will certainly come to a stop, very soon.'

And that was all she would say, to Tim, and his startled parents, as she made a polite but speedy departure.

'We don't know if she's coming back,' Tim's mother said, 'or anything!'

'At least she didn't charge us,' Tim's father chuckled.

Tim felt a bit crushed. Lethe seemed so nice, and they got on so well . . . But she'd just rushed off as if she wasn't interested any more.

That night his sleep was broken by one of the worst nightmares ever. A stooping thing that writhed horribly under its cloak, whose face—briefly glimpsed—seemed to be slimy and scaly, with jutting jaws that formed a grisly beak. And after storming around the room, that monster wheeled towards Tim, hissing, with a crooked hand reaching from the cloak, talons glinting . . .

But to Tim's total astonishment, it was halted—by another being, appearing from nowhere in front of the clawed horror.

A small, slim being, wearing a short gauzy robe. A being whose skin was covered by a web-like network of fine green lines, faintly glowing.

The being spoke briefly to the cloaked monster, in a strange musical language, and the monster hissed and disappeared. Then the small one turned to Tim—who nearly fell out of bed in shock.

'Lethe!' he gasped.

'Yes, Tim,' she said, smiling, the green lines glowing on her face. 'This is how I truly am—without all that make-up. Do not be afraid.'

'I'm not,' Tim said. 'Not now. How did you get into my dream?'

'You are not dreaming,' she told him. 'None of your times of terror have been dreams. They have been moments when . . . when real creatures crossed over from where they should have been, into your room.'

'How?' Tim asked, frowning. 'And where should they have been?'

Lethe sighed. 'It is not easy to explain . . . There is something like an enormous *transport* system, Tim, stretching further than you can imagine. Those who travel on it are first reduced to basic particles, within a force field. Then they are transported, *instantly*, along energy lines, and restored.'

'Like the way people are *beamed up*, in *Star Trek*?' Tim suggested.

'Perhaps,' Lethe said. 'I do not know *Star Trek*.'

'So . . . where *is* this transport system?' Tim asked, though he had already guessed.

'Among the stars,' she said. 'Linking thousands of planets.'

'Then the monsters weren't ghosts or demons!' Tim cried. 'They were *aliens*!'

'To you, yes,' she smiled. 'As am I.'

'And the thing in my wall wasn't a magic amulet . . . ' Tim added.

She laughed softly. 'No. It was one of the millions of power nodes that hold the lines of energy together, for the transport system. When you displaced it, the energy line broke at this point.'

'Sorry,' Tim mumbled.

'You could not have known,' Lethe said gently. 'But it meant that the travellers were restored too soon—not at their destinations, but in your bedroom.'

'That's why they seemed so angry,' Tim said. 'And they were probably looking for the amulet . . . the node thing. Why did they all wear cloaks?'

'Those are protective garments,' Lethe said, 'in case they arrive in the wrong place, somewhere that is dangerous to them. That can happen, now and then.'

Tim frowned again. 'So . . . before, when the amulet, the node, was in my wall—all sorts of aliens must have been flying through my room, along the energy line, all the time!'

Lethe laughed again. 'But moving in a way that you would never notice—in the form of energy impulses, sixty billion times faster than the speed of light.'

Tim gulped, almost speechless with amazement. 'What will happen?' he asked. 'Can it be fixed?'

'That is why I am here,' Lethe said. 'It took time to find the exact node that had gone wrong—and I am sorry, Tim, that you were so troubled in that time. But your bad dreams led me to you, and now I can replace the node.'

'Back in my wall?' Tim asked, a bit nervously.

'No,' she said. 'Somewhere near, but out of the way. Come.'

As she took his hand, the eerie green lines on her skin flared. Suddenly, to Tim's astonishment, they were on the roof of the house, beside the chimney.

From somewhere in her robe Lethe took another flat tablet wrapped in thin metal. She reached out towards the chimney, the lines on her arm glowing like green fire—and her hand, holding the tablet, sank smoothly into the brickwork.

When she drew her hand out, it was empty. 'That restores the energy line,' she said softly, then took his hand again—and at once he was back in bed.

'You may sleep peacefully now, Tim,' Lethe murmured, touching his cheek, 'and forget all those terrors. Farewell.'

Then she was gone. And as her touch sent Tim drifting into sleep, he smiled to himself.

Forget? Not a chance, he thought. Even the Shadow-Master never met anyone like Lethe . . .

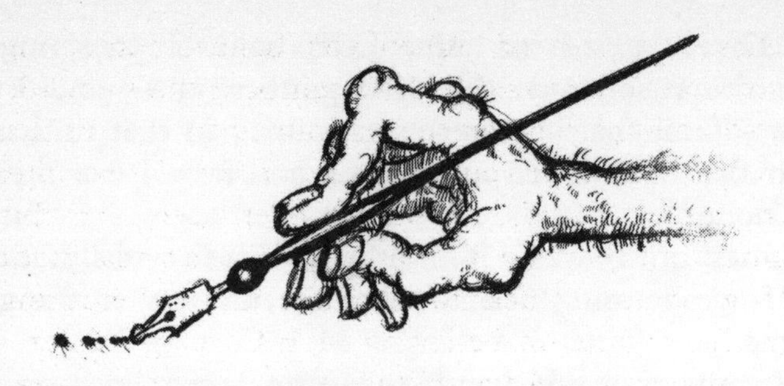

Sarah

ALISON PRINCE

I didn't think there were any mysteries, not any more. I'd known for ages that all the stuff they tell you when you're small is a load of rubbish. You kind of know it is, even at the time, but you don't like to say. The tooth fairy, for instance. If it was really a fairy, you wouldn't be able to argue about how much a tooth is worth. You'd just find a silver sixpence or something—not real money. I started on fifty pence, then found out most people got a pound and grumbled to Mum about it, so next time I got a pound, too. From the tooth fairy. But it's nice of parents to take the trouble, and you don't want to spoil it for them. Same with Father Christmas and the reindeer and stuff.

Part of it's OK, like hanging up your stocking. You can't help getting a buzz, knowing there's going to be that lumpy weight on the end of your bed in the morning. It's obviously not put there by F.C. and the reindeer—I mean, with central heating and double glazing, it's a ridiculous idea—but I used to like kidding myself there was a bit of magic going on. And

I believed it, sort of. When you believe something, it doesn't have to be *real* real. It can be a different sort of real, something you can see in your head even if there's nothing to see with your eyes. A bit like the pictures in books for little kids. Nobody's ever seen a rabbit in pyjamas, but there he is, real because he's a real picture.

If we'd just stuck to hanging up the stocking, I might have gone on believing in F.C. a bit longer, but the trouble was, Mum and Dad took to smuggling my bigger presents into my bedroom as well. I suppose they thought it kept me busy for longer in the morning, so they got a bit of a lie-in. I could see their point. But one year they gave me a snare-drum.

It wasn't their fault. I'd been pestering for it, I admit that. Dad's a drummer with a band called the Clarkston Cats (that's where we live, Clarkston), and I was desperate to play drums like him. He let me use his kit occasionally, but a lot of the time it was in the van, packed up in its cases ready for a gig. And anyway, he said it was best to get my basic rhythm going on a single snare-drum. So in the middle of the night that Christmas, he and Mum lugged this thing in, wrapped in a lot of paper and tied up with red ribbon. But you can't shut a snare-drum up. The grid of wires across it clicks and hisses every time you touch it, and Mum had got the giggles and Dad kept whispering, 'Shut up!' I was trying hard to pretend I was asleep, but they knew I wasn't, because I had the giggles, too. So that was it, really. Goodbye, F.C. After the snare-drum, I really couldn't kid myself I believed in him any more.

A whole lot of other fairy-tales got debunked as well. I found out where babies came from and why Mr Beveridge up the road wasn't allowed to drive his car for a year, and why Mum wouldn't speak to Auntie

Doris. (They'd quarrelled over who should have Granny's gardening hat when she died. I don't know why they wanted it, neither of them are the sort for tatty pink rosebuds, but there you are.) One way and another, I thought I was pretty clued-up about what was real and what wasn't.

Then this new girl came to school. Her name was Sarah. She had fair hair, parted in the middle, and she looked very clean and kind of *good*. Nobody thought she was much fun, but she stuck up for me one day when Miss Armitage threw a fit about me using my mobile phone, so I quite liked her. A lot of people didn't. They said she was weird because her parents belonged to a batty religious lot who met in a tin-roofed hut down by the railway station on Sundays. Sarah never said anything about it, and neither did I, so that was fine.

One day I mentioned that Dad's band was going to be playing on local radio. A DJ who ran a programme called *Turning Up Music* had been in Clarkston, helping a mate to move out. They saw one of the Cats' posters in the pub, and the DJ went to their next gig and thought they were pretty good. I was dead excited, of course. 'Talk about luck!' I said.

Sarah shook her head and said, 'There's no such thing as luck.'

I couldn't see what she meant. I said it was obvious there was luck. Nobody could make things happen the way they wanted, they just had to put up with what arrived. You never knew what was coming.

'But God knows,' Sarah said. 'He's in charge of everything. That's why you have to pray. It's not luck, it's what He decides for us.'

I could tell she'd put a capital H on *He*, because of the way she said it.

I didn't know what to say. She wasn't joking—she was absolutely serious. It was a bit embarrassing, really. I mean, you don't expect people to come out with stuff like that, quite casually, when you're sharing a packet of crisps.

I thought about it all afternoon, while we were doing stuff about rainforests. I didn't know much about God—it wasn't a subject that had ever cropped up at home. I'd walked past churches, of course, and seen how they usually had a notice board outside saying *Jesus Saves* or something like that, but I'd always thought it was a message for people who belonged to the church, like members of a club. They'd understand what it meant. Being saved sounded a bit frightening, now I came to think about it. Saved from what? I started to wonder if I'd done something wrong that I didn't know about, or if there was a dreadfulness all round that I couldn't see but had to be rescued from.

Jesus and God weren't like Father Christmas, that you grew out of. Even grown-ups were supposed to be very respectful about them. Gran used to have a picture of Jesus on the dining room wall, with lot of sheep all round him, and a halo. I could see Jesus was very kind to the sheep, and it worried me a bit when we had roast lamb, but I never said anything. Gran liked people to have good manners and clean hands, and that seemed something to do with God as well, or Jesus, or both. But as for the rest—it was a mystery.

I went on thinking about it as I walked home. If Sarah was right and there really was no such thing as luck, then there was no point in thinking you had any choice. It was all fixed. God could be a complete system, like a giant computer, and we might be just small parts of it, not free to make up our own minds at all. It was a scary idea.

I asked Mum if she thought God organized everything, and she looked a bit startled and said, 'Difficult to say, isn't it. I think everyone has to make up their own mind.' Which wasn't a lot of help, really.

By the time I went to bed, I'd got a bad dose of the heebies. I kept imagining there was a giant eye up there in the night sky, staring down at me through the ceiling of my bedroom and the roof above it as if they'd gone transparent. I pulled the duvet over my head, but the eye could see through the duvet and through my pyjamas, right in to my shrinking, naked self. It was awful. I began to see why Sarah thought you have to pray. I felt like a helpless little worm that some huge scientist was staring at. He could squash me whenever he wanted to, or else be kind and make me warm and comfortable—but either way, he did the choosing. I could only squeak as loud as I could and hope he took some notice. If he even heard.

The next morning, I was still bothered. I wanted to write God off as an invention by grown-ups that I didn't have to think about, but I wasn't sure. And if God really was up there, running things, he had some pretty funny ways of going about it.

As soon as I got to school, I found Sarah and said, 'Listen, what about all the stuff on the telly? People starving to death and being blown up, and maniacs flying planes into buildings—if God's in charge, why does that happen?'

'People are sinful,' she said. 'They don't do God's will. That's why you have to pray, in case you're getting it wrong without knowing.'

I gave up. Her argument only worked if you believed it. If you didn't, then there was no point. And I didn't know if I believed it or not. I did a lot of drum practice for the next evening or two, so as to stop thinking about God. It drives you batty, trying to get your head round that sort of thing.

A week or two later, there was another stroke of luck, or whatever Sarah would call it. Only this time, it was a really big one. The Three-legged Pigs were coming to play at the Town Hall.

Everyone was desperate to get tickets. We'd all seen The Pigs on TV—they're absolutely brilliant. Sarah was dying to go. Even though she looked so neat and good, she was as keen as anyone else when it came to a treat like that. But her parents didn't do anything about getting tickets. Maybe they weren't into rock music—I wouldn't know. But when I admitted that I was going, she looked all droopy, as if she'd cry at any moment. 'Oh,' she said, 'you're so lucky.' And I felt so sorry for her, I didn't make any smart comments.

My dad had got tickets through the Pigs' drummer, Buddy McKenzie, because Buddy had started him off on the drums when he'd just left school and they were both working for the Gas Board. I didn't spread this around, because everyone would think I was showing off. I just said the tickets were bought through the Internet, which was almost true, except it was an e-mail to Buddy. But Dad warned me to shut up about it. The concert had sold out like lightning, and if I once let on that Dad knew someone in the Pigs, we'd have everyone pestering him to do them a favour. But I did ask him if he could get a ticket for Sarah.

He smiled. 'Is she your girlfriend?' he asked.

I didn't like to say she wasn't, so I just said, 'Sort of,' and turned a bit red because it's awful when grown-ups start on that sort of thing. And Dad patted me on the shoulder and said he'd see what he could do.

A couple of days later, another ticket came through the post. I took it to school, safe in its envelope. I felt terrific, like Father Christmas with a sackful of gifts. This was a piece of sheer, beautiful luck, and it had changed everything. I'd chosen to do something nice for Sarah, and I'd been lucky—it had worked. It might not have done, but it had. As I walked along the road, the sky seemed wonderfully clear, full of lovely chances and free of any watchful eye.

I found Sarah in the playground, standing with her hands in her pockets and looking miserable. She turned away when she saw me, the lucky guy who was going to the concert, but I went up to her and said, 'Hi!'

I still kick myself that I didn't simply give her the ticket and shut up. But I was so happy at having something marvellous for her, and so relieved that luck really existed, I wanted to tease her. So I said, 'Have you been praying for a ticket?'

Sarah shook her head and didn't smile. 'You can't expect God to bother about things like that,' she said. 'And anyway there's no point, there aren't any tickets. They've all gone.'

'Oh, no, they haven't!' I took the ticket out of my pocket, slipped it out of its brown envelope and showed it to her. 'It's for you,' I told her, and put it in her hand.

She stared down at it as if she couldn't believe it. And then I put the finishing touches to my big mistake. 'It wasn't God, you see,' I said, beaming like an idiot. 'It was me. And luck. Pure luck.'

Her face crumpled. Her nose turned pink, and tears welled up in her blue eyes. 'I hate you!' she shouted. 'You're just—wicked!' And she pushed the ticket back at me and ran.

I tried several times that day to say I was sorry, but Sarah was surrounded by a group of girls who had suddenly become her friends and walked about hugging her, and they all looked at me as if I was a monster. I don't know what she'd told them, they just said over their shoulders that I'd been horrible to her.

It left me with a big problem about the ticket. I couldn't face telling Dad what had happened, but I'd have to cook up some reason why Sarah wasn't going to come after all. That meant I'd have to invent a story. Tell a lie. I trailed home in absolute misery. Sarah was right, I'd been wicked. I shouldn't have teased her about something that she thought was so important. And because I had, I'd got myself into this awful mess.

There was something else, too. Perhaps God was at work, after all. He might have organized the whole thing so as to teach me not to be so cocky. Behind the scenes, he could have been making sure there was a spare ticket for Sarah, and fixed it so I had the chance to be nice to her. Maybe it was all a kind of test, and I'd blown it. But why hadn't Sarah seen it that way? OK, I'd blown the test—but she'd blown it, too. If she was serious about God, she ought to have believed he could get her a ticket. She could have prayed, but she didn't. So maybe she had been wicked as well.

It was all extremely difficult. And what was worse, I knew I had to tell this whacking great lie. I'd decided to say Sarah's parents had fixed up to take her to something else, to make up for the disappointment of missing the concert. And she couldn't let them down. It had to be a really artistic lie.

Dad was very nice about it. He asked if I'd like to take anyone else instead, but I shook my head. So we ended up with Mrs Prosser from next door, who sat with her hands over her ears most of the time and said it was terribly loud.

The Pigs were great, of course, but all the way through the concert, I kept thinking about the lie I'd told, and about being horrible to Sarah, and the eye of God seemed to be looking down through the high ceiling of the hall, watching me. If he chose, he could send a thunderbolt through the roof or cause the electrics on the stage to blow up and fry everyone. My hands were sweating, and not just because of the crowd and the lights.

I was relieved to get out unpunished and unharmed, though I worried a bit about the crush of people going out of the doors, and wondered if I was fated to trip and get trampled underfoot. All the way home in the car, I was scared that someone would shoot a traffic light and crash into us, or that Dad would have a heart attack and die at the wheel, though none of it was his fault.

We got home OK. The house wasn't on fire and the cat hadn't been run over, and things seemed completely normal.

They still do, more or less. I heard at school the next day that Sarah had fallen off her bike on the evening of the concert and broken her arm. That bothered me for quite a bit, but I've stopped thinking about it now. I reckon there are some things I'll never understand.

It could be just a question of what to call them.

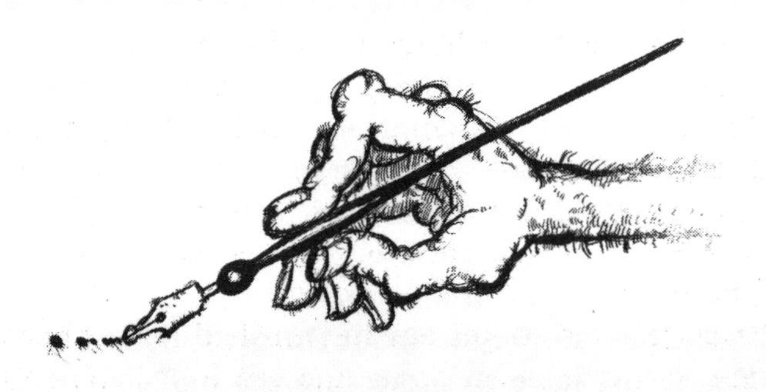

Doing the Bank

JAN BURCHETT and SARA VOGLER

I pushed open the doors. I knew what I had to do, and no one was going to stop me. I swaggered up to the man in black. I could see he didn't like me. That was fine. I didn't like him. But I knew I was safe. My library books may have been three days overdue but he couldn't touch me for it. Kids don't get fined in our library.

I stuck the books right under his nose and set off for the crime section. I could devour three or four thrillers a week and never forget a word. It had made me the best private investigator in town. Well, that and changing my name. If you've been christened Arnold Cheesebottom you've got to find a new handle—and fast. So I did. Mack Mason, that's me, up and running and ready for my first big case. Until now it had all been kids' stuff, like finding the missing supply teacher in the cupboard last week. And discovering who'd eaten Daisy Carter's sandwiches. And tracking down the culprit who'd put a muddy football in the rice pudding.

It was quiet in the library. Too quiet. There was

something fishy going on. I could hear whispers. I parted a couple of whodunits and peered through the gap. There were two men in the next aisle. One was tall, with a dark beard. The other had shifty eyes.

'This could be difficult,' muttered the Beard.

'I thought it was all sorted,' answered Shifty. 'She said get the guppies, didn't she?'

'Yeah, but she forgot about the mad molly.'

'You'll just have to make sure the molly's out of the way.'

Criminals always use code. And this was a clever one. I knew they weren't really talking about tropical fish. I'd stumbled on a mystery, right here in the crime section. Or next to it anyway.

The Beard's mobile rang. He answered it furtively.

'Yes, guv,' he muttered. 'We're in the library . . . yeah, we know we're doing the bank. OK, guv.' He pocketed the mobile and nodded at Shifty. 'Let's go!'

They left. But not before I'd had a good look at them. I'd remember them again in a dark bank vault.

I leant against the murder mysteries and thought about what I'd heard. One—these guys were going to rob a bank of all its guppies—that must be criminal code for money. Two—they were doing it today. Three—the mad molly was out of the way. That must be the bank manager. This was a case for Mack Mason, private investigator. There wasn't much to go on, but one thing was sure—I knew which bank. It had to be the Countrywide in the High Street. How did I know? Because knowing was my business. It was big, it was busy, and it was the only bank in town. But foiling a bank robbery was too much for one boy alone—even for such a skilled detective as me. I needed help and there was only one person I could trust. My friend Gizmo, sidekick and gadget maker supreme.

Five minutes later Gizmo and I were on our way to the bank. It was eleven hundred hours and the place was full of hardworking citizens about their business. We skulked in a corner by the deposit forms. Sure enough Shifty and the Beard were there. We could see their game straight away. They were posing as decorators. It was a clever ruse but I could see they weren't professionals. There's a knack to opening a pot of paint—and they didn't have it. The door to the back was propped open with a tin of Almond White. We could see right out to the back door where their van was waiting. They had it all worked out. Slap a bit of paint around, wait till the coast was clear, and steal the money. It was time to speak to the man in charge. Keeping the decorators in my sights, I strolled over to what looked like a junior clerk, fresh out of training. She was spending more time watching the decorators than doing any work herself. I decided to shake her up.

'Excuse me, miss,' I said crisply. 'I need to speak to the manager.'

She smiled.

'I'm Miss Deedes,' she said. 'Manager of this branch. What can I do for you?'

So this was the mad molly! You could have knocked me down with a warrant card. This young slip of a thing was the manager of a huge bank? She looked more like she was standing in for her dad. But a top private investigator never loses his cool. I gave her the low-down. She looked worried.

'Don't worry, ma'am,' I said. 'Mack Mason's on the case.' Gizmo coughed loudly. 'Oh . . . and Gizmo. We know the next step—call the cops.'

I could see Ms Deedes was impressed.

'That would be a very good idea, Mr Mason . . . and Mr Gizmo,' she said eventually, 'if we had some hard evidence. But we don't. Thanks for the tip off. I'll see you out.'

'Not so fast, ma'am.' I held up a hand. 'We're not going anywhere until these men are under lock and key.'

'And I wanted to use my new home-made two-way radio,' added Gizmo, rummaging in his jacket pocket. 'I'll show you. It's got—'

'Shut it, Gizmo.'

'OK, boss.'

'We're at your service, ma'am,' I said reassuringly.

'I can see you boys mean business,' said Ms Deedes. This dame recognized top investigators when she saw them. 'I suggest you set up an observation right here in the lobby. Keep an eye on the decorators. And make sure you stay here. Don't go poking about!'

We took up our surveillance positions. I squatted behind a pot plant. Gizmo was under the grow-your-own-pension stand. We kept in constant touch via the two-way radios. It wasn't easy. When your handset's a converted cheese grater it's hard on the ears. For a long time there was nothing to report. Then it happened. On the stroke of twelve the decorators downed tools. They sauntered towards the propped open door, whistling casually. This was obviously a signal. I knew where they were heading. They were making for the vaults, and the dough—that's money in normalspeak.

'All systems go!' I growled into the cheese grater.

Gizmo leapt up. He'd forgotten he was under the stand. By the time we'd picked up the pension leaflets the men had gone. We ran to follow but when we reached the door there was no sign of them. Gizmo pulled a small wooden box from his pocket.

'It detects body heat,' he explained. 'If this doesn't find them, nothing will.'

'Good thinking, Gizmo.'

'Thanks, boss.'

As we crept along past filing cabinets and photocopiers, the box bleeped efficiently. We turned a corner and it blew a raspberry. It had found its target. The wrong target. Ms Deedes was standing with her back to us in front of an open vault. And it was empty.

'Scrap the detector, Gizmo,' I muttered.

'Right, boss.'

I strode up to the bank manager, stepping over a bulging briefcase as I went.

'Don't worry, Ms Deedes,' I said. She jumped like a hog on a hotplate. 'We're here to help. Those decorators won't get far.'

Ms Deedes looked relieved. It was lucky for her that someone with my expertise was on the spot.

'We both know the drill, ma'am,' I told her. 'We must call the p—'

'We must get away!' Ms Deedes interrupted.

'Get away?' gasped Gizmo.

'Erm . . . of course,' said the bank manager hurriedly. 'There's no time to call the police. We must go . . . in case the robbers come back! We're . . . er . . . witnesses. They'll want to silence us. Quick! My car's out the back.'

She went to pick up her briefcase. I stepped in.

'Allow me, ma'am,' I said. I gave it a heave. I could hardly move it.

'Just some bank papers I need to look at,' said Ms Deedes, in a fluster. This was one hardworking woman. She hustled us to the door. Gizmo and I staggered out with the briefcase. There was no sign of the decorators' van. We followed the bank manager across the car park to a blue hatchback.

'Get in,' she said grimly.

We clambered into the back with the briefcase between us and she sped off with a screech of tyres. Gizmo pulled a contraption from his pocket. It was his homemade bean can periscope. He kept watch with it out of the back window as we went. We hadn't gone far when he grabbed my arm.

'I can see something! I think it's a UFO!'

This was a new twist. I hadn't dealt with aliens before. I grabbed the periscope and took a look.

'It's a baked bean, you dingbat!' I snorted. 'You didn't wash the tin out.'

'Sorry, boss.'

I flicked the offending bean out of the window and Gizmo took up his surveillance again. We sped on through the town.

'They're behind us!' shouted Gizmo. 'Hide!'

He slid down in his seat, thrusting the periscope into my hand. I had a casual look. It was probably a blob of tomato sauce this time. But he was right! The decorators' van was close on our tail.

'Hold on to your seats, boys,' muttered Ms Deedes, looking wildly in her mirror.

We had to lose them—and fast. We roared down the High Street and spun past Pets-u-like into Station Lane. Ms Deedes slammed the gas pedal to the floor and we zoomed over a zebra crossing just as a bunch of four-years-olds were about to put their toes on the stripes. It was a good move. The decorator's van came to a halt as the whole nursery school toddled across in a crocodile line. We'd lost them.

We took the next corner on two wheels and sped past a parked police car. One of the cops inside was talking on his radio. The squad car's siren immediately burst into life and it began to follow, its blue light flashing.

'The police are tailing us,' announced Gizmo, adjusting his periscope.

'Why would the cops be tailing us, Gizmo?' I hissed. 'We're the good guys.'

'So what are they doing?'

'Just ignore them!' snapped Ms Deedes, as we tore down the slip road to the bypass.

'They're protecting us, you numskull!' I explained. 'They're giving us an escort, isn't that right, ma'am?'

'Escort!' spluttered the bank manager. 'Yes, of course . . . that's right. An escort.'

The escort had trouble keeping up as Ms Deedes swung in and out of the traffic. Horns were sounding and drivers were shaking their fists. We ignored them all. They'd feel silly tomorrow when they saw our story in the paper and found they'd hooted the great Mack Mason.

Ms Deedes suddenly veered off down an exit. We read the signpost as we flashed past.

'Why are we heading for the airport?' asked Gizmo.

'Witness protection, I imagine,' I said grimly. 'We have to go abroad. Assume a new identity.'

'Cool!' gasped Gizmo. 'Hang on a minute. Won't we need passports?' That was the trouble with Gizmo. Too many questions and not enough answers.

'The cops will have that sorted,' I said knowledgeably. The police were now waving at us through their open windows and one officer, who had his head poking through the sunroof, was yelling into a megaphone. I gave them a smart salute.

We were doing seventy-five round a corner when a tractor and trailer suddenly appeared on the road ahead of us. Ms Deedes slammed on the brakes, but we were still heading straight for its rear end. Then, just when I thought our number was up, she swerved to overtake with a skilful flick of the wheel. But then she made her big mistake. We cut in sharply—too sharply. The tractor was forced off the road into a hedge and the trailer hit a boulder and shed its steaming load of manure all over the police car.

'It's OK, boys,' said Ms Deedes as we turned into the airport. 'We can manage from here without them.'

'Haven't they got our passports?' asked Gizmo.

Ms Deedes didn't answer. We screeched to a halt next to a no parking sign right in front of the main doors.

'Quick, boys,' she yelled as she got out, 'give me my briefcase. And stay put.'

We heaved the case over to her. She staggered off with it towards the airport lounge and disappeared through the revolving glass doors.

'What do we do now, boss?' asked Gizmo, folding up his periscope.

'Simple,' I said. 'We stay here like she told us.' I leaned back and put my feet up. 'You know, Gizmo, this is our best mission yet. It's even better than the time I solved the case of the Hound of the Junior School.'

'That was a good one, boss,' said Gizmo.

'Plenty of evidence—the mauled maths book, the paw print in the plasticine, the screams from the office.'

'Yes,' agreed Gizmo. 'You weren't to know the head had brought her puppy in for the day.'

At that moment a van pulled up behind us. It was the robbers! The two men jumped out of the cab, took one look at Ms Deedes's car and sprinted into the airport lounge. In the distance we could hear a police car siren. The cops would never get here in time.

'It's up to us, Gizmo,' I declared. 'We've got to protect the lady.'

We scrambled out of the car and followed the decorators through the doors. After five revolutions we found ourselves in the hustle and bustle of a busy airport. We scanned the faces. At last we spotted Ms Deedes. She was at the check-in desk. She must be sorting out our tickets. The robbers had almost reached her! Saving the dame and beating the bad guys is all in a day's work for a private investigator.

'Get them, Gizmo!' I yelled.

We ploughed through the crowd and made for the decorators. I grabbed a wastepaper bin, leapt on to the Beard's back and stuck it over his head. Gizmo clamped himself to Shifty's leg. They wouldn't be going anywhere in a hurry.

'What's going on?' came the Beard's muffled voice.

'Get off!' wailed Shifty, shaking his leg.

'Run, Ms Deedes,' I yelled. 'Don't worry about us.'

Ms Deedes hoiked up her bag. She made for the departure gate. At least one of us would get away. Suddenly there was a commotion in the crowd. People backed off, holding their noses, as three manure-covered policemen marched through.

'Over here, officers,' I called. 'We've caught the villains!'

But the damp and steaming cops went straight after Ms Deedes. It was obvious why. One—they could see I had the situation in hand. Two—they wanted the whole story. Three—they knew I'd be too modest to tell them.

Ms Deedes didn't seem to realize they were policemen. I wasn't surprised. There was too much muck and not enough uniform showing. She swung her briefcase at the nearest one. He ducked, but it floored his colleague. The third cop stepped forward and slipped on a pile of dung that had plopped off his trousers.

Now there was only one officer left standing. He grabbed at her arm. This time Ms Deedes didn't miss. She whammed the guy right in the belly with the briefcase. He went flying and the case burst open. The whole airport stood in amazement as a shower of fifty-pound notes filled the air. I had to hand it to the robbers. They were smarter than I thought. Somehow they had planted the stolen cash in the bank manager's briefcase!

Shifty was the first to move. With Gizmo sliding behind him, still gripping his leg for grim death, he shuffled across and took her by the arm.

'Melanie Deedes,' he announced solemnly, flashing a warrant card at her. 'I am arresting you for the bank robbery at the Countrywide Bank.' And, from the pocket of his paint-stained overalls, he produced a pair of handcuffs and clamped them round her wrists. This robber was cool. Impersonating a police officer was a serious offence in my book.

It was up to me to sort things out. I climbed down the Beard's back and marched up to the real cops.

'Pardon me, officers,' I began, 'I think you'll find . . . '

But nobody was listening. One policeman was peeling banknotes off his steaming uniform. A second one grovelled about picking up the rest of the scattered money. The third one went over to the Beard and whipped the bin off his head.

'Might have known it would be you two,' he sneered. 'Call yourselves plain-clothes detectives?'

'You can talk!' said the Beard, squinting in the light. 'Who lost Deedes on the airport approach road?'

'It's difficult tailing a suspect when you've got a car full of dung. Anyway, you two shouldn't have left the bank in the first place.'

'I had to pick up my new tropical fish,' protested the Beard. 'We caught up with her in town though.'

'You soon lost her again!'

'I couldn't go too fast,' explained the Beard. 'I had the guppies in the back of the van. Baby fish can't have too much excitement, you know.'

The officer looked interested.

'You got guppies? How are they going to get on with that mad molly of yours? It's a dangerous fish, that one. It might eat them!'

'I know. It was the wife's idea . . . '

'Excuse me, gentlemen,' interrupted Ms Deedes, impatiently. 'Could you get on with arresting me, please? I haven't got all day.'

I watched as the uniformed cops escorted her away. So Ms Deedes had robbed her own bank and the decorators were undercover police. I'd known it all along. I looked down at my sidekick.

'You can let go of the detective's leg now, Gizmo. I've solved the case.'

'Have you, boss?' said Gizmo, jumping to his feet.

'I sure have.' I turned to the Beard. 'We'd be happy to accompany you to the station house for a debriefing, officer. Mack Mason always has the facts at his fingertips.'

'I bet you do,' said Shifty, putting a heavy hand on our shoulders.

'Too right,' growled the Beard. 'First, let's hear about assaulting a police officer with a wastepaper bin . . . '

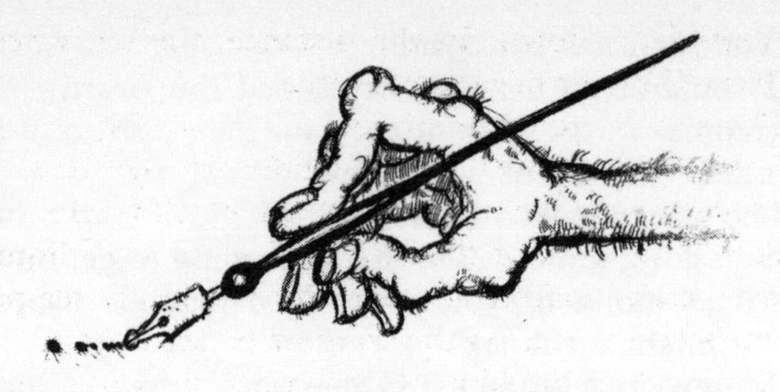

Mysteries

LAURENCE STAIG

Mr Ligotti paused and stared about the room. He fixed his pupils with a stone-grey stare and held his hand in the air, as though it were a claw. Some members of the class allowed nervous laughs to escape into the moment of silence. Most remained perfectly still and watched their new favourite teacher. Mr Ligotti had once been a priest in Rome. For some reason he had left the priesthood and become a teacher. Every lesson was a performance. He was strange—but fun.

'For homework and to finish off in class today, I asked you to make a list of amazing things. Things of which there appears to be no known explanation! *I fantastico!* Mysteries!'

Pupils in the front row shifted in their seats.

'Are things what they seem?' exclaimed Mr Ligotti. He twisted his head towards the window where distant storm clouds had begun to roll across the sky.

'What is out there?' he asked.

A far off crackle of lightning echoed above the

rooftops of the town. In the distance, the big wheel of the travelling fair began to revolve.

The class were mesmerized.

Jenny looked over her shoulder at the new boy, wondering what he thought of all of this. He sat in silence at the back of the room. His eyes were liquid—almost dark marble pools. A gentle pitter-patter commenced its beat on the window panes.

'Stop staring at him,' Susan said, nudging Jenny's arm.

'Tell us about one of *your* mysteries, Jenny,' said Mr Ligotti, his smile wider than a crocodile's.

Jenny glanced at Susan. She looked blank before finding the right page in her exercise book.

'I've . . . I've always been interested in monsters,' she began.

'Ah,' said Mr Ligotti, his mouth opening into a cavernous 'O'. 'The monster! In Italy we say—*il mostro!* And what kind might they be?'

'Well, I chose to do something on the Loch Ness monster. We went on holiday last year to Scotland and visited Loch Ness.'

'And did you see the monster?' asked Mr Ligotti.

'Well, not exactly,' replied Jenny.

'Not exactly?' repeated Mr Ligotti with one of his big frowns. 'What does that mean? Come on now, don't tease us so, tell us more.'

'Well, my dad thought he saw something. It was in the far part of the loch, a dark shadowy thing with humps. We got in the car and drove around the coast road to get a better look.'

There was silence you could almost smell.

'Go on,' said Mr Ligotti.

Susan cast a sidelong glance at Jenny. 'Well, when we got around the other side we looked around and there was no sign of it. Then . . . then Mum discovered a line of old tree trunks, they'd drifted into the water and were bobbing about on the surface.'

The class moaned with disappointment.

'Things were not as they appeared then?' said Mr Ligotti, with one of his serious looks.

Suddenly, a small voice spoke up from a desk beside the far wall. Billy, a small pug-nosed boy with cropped hair, grinned.

'I like dragons!'

'Do you, now?' said Mr Ligotti.

'Vikings used to paint dragons on their shields,' Billy continued, almost panting to get his information out. 'And they had dragons on the front bits of their ships too!'

'Prow,' said Mr Ligotti. '*Prow* of their ships—good boy, Billy.'

'But there's no such things as dragons,' said Jenny, irritably.

'And no such thing as Loch Ness monsters either!' Billy snapped back.

'What about werewolves?' someone said.

'Sir? Do angels exist, sir?' asked Melanie, a round-faced girl with wire-framed spectacles.

Mr Ligotti turned on his heels and caught his breath. Then after a moment he held up his hands.

'Class, class. Calm. These are all mysteries, but sadly, as we know, there is little evidence for all these wonderful and incredible sounding creatures.' For a moment Mr Ligotti went quiet again as though he had become thoughtful. 'I . . . I mean to say, I've never seen a photograph of a dragon! I've yet to have many things proven to me . . . Such things do not exist!'

He gave a kindly smile. He was unsure how to

answer Melanie's question about the angel. Billy looked disappointed. Somewhere, somebody sighed.

'I've some pictures.'

The comment came from the shadows, from the back of the room. There was an Irish lilt, a gentle sing-song in the voice. Jenny twisted round. She knew who it would be. It was Sean, the new boy. As usual he sat very still—reserved and dignified. For a moment he tossed his fringe to the side.

'Why, Sean, our fairground family visitor,' said Mr Ligotti. 'Bravo, it is so good that you are joining in. You've pictures, have you?'

Sean nodded. 'Of things.'

'Of *things*?' said Mr Ligotti. 'Now what things might that be?'

Sean did not reply.

Mr Ligotti stared at him. The boy said nothing, but stared back.

'Things?' Mr Ligotti repeated.

Sean reached down and produced a crumpled brown paper bag. He placed the bag on his desk and held Mr Ligotti's gaze. For a moment the silence was as electric as the brewing storm.

'Pictures?' repeated Mr Ligotti. He crossed the floor and looked down at Sean's bag.

'Photographs. They are my grandfather's,' said Sean. 'There's only a few, we lost the rest in a fire last year when we were at the Tewsbury Goose Fair.'

Mr Ligotti placed a single finger on the bag and twisted it round, so that the opening was towards him. All eyes were on the pair. It was as if some kind of challenge had been thrown down. Jenny and Susan watched carefully, Jenny narrowing her eyes.

'OK, signor.' Mr Ligotti sprang to life. 'Let's take a look, then.'

Sean lifted up the bag and allowed several crumpled black and white photographs, of various sizes, to fall out on to the desk top. Mr Ligotti peered down at them. Behind him there was the sound of shuffling, as eager pupils strained to see.

Mr Ligotti picked up the largest of the pictures, which was about the size of a pair of postcards. He said nothing for a moment, then put the picture back on the desk. He glanced at Sean as he picked up another.

'What are they, sir?' said Jenny, unable to stand the suspense any longer. She put her blonde hair behind her ears and edged forward.

Again Mr Ligotti looked at Sean and picked up another picture. He was clearly fascinated, but he had also become quiet and serious.

'Perhaps *you* could tell us, Sean?'

Sean blinked. 'Like I told you, they belong to Grandfather, he looks after me. They're pictures from his old Travelling Show. He used to tour it everywhere, but not these days. Says people wouldn't understand. Most of the exhibits were burned in this fire I told you about. We've some left though.' Then he added. 'I thought this was right—for what you wanted us to do?'

Mr Ligotti nodded. 'Most interesting, in fact *very* interesting. My—they are so convincing, though one or two are a bit—how you say—dodgy on quality.'

'That's because they're old,' said Sean.

'Oh, sir, please!' somebody called from the back of the gathering cluster of children. A flash of thunder lit up the room.

Mr Ligotti gathered up the photographs and stepped across to his table. He cleared away the piles of books and carefully laid the pictures out on the surface.

'We'll take it in turns,' he said. 'Now—the first two rows.'

Anxious bodies, all arms and legs, clambered over the desks and chairs to Mr Ligotti's table. Jenny picked up the large photograph and looked at it. The picture appeared to have been taken inside a tent, as there was a background of stripes. On a table lay the figure of a girl. She had long blonde hair which reached down to her waist. Her eyes were closed and she looked very beautiful. It was at the waist that things changed. For instead of legs, a silvery pattern of scales appeared to surface from the skin. From here they narrowed to a fish's tail.

'It's a mermaid . . . ' Jenny whispered.

She smiled but then frowned. She held the photograph closer. It was very convincing. She looked up at Sean, who now stood beside Mr Ligotti.

'Cleverly done,' said Mr Ligotti, as he cleared his throat. 'This was a kind of side-show then, we had many of them back in Italy—travelling shows, yes?'

Sean nodded. 'Gramps made them.'

'*Made them!*' repeated Mr Ligotti. 'Ah, I see! An artist, a true artist. What are they made of, I wonder. Some kind of resin or perhaps paper mâché and wire, I think?'

Sean stood in silence.

By now the rest of the class had forgotten Mr Ligotti's instructions about taking turns; a mound of children, balanced on chairs and desk tops, had grown just above the table.

Susan held a picture in front of her face and looked over the top of it at Sean. He remained beside Mr Ligotti. Jenny squeezed through to her friend and looked over her shoulder.

'It's shining—an incredible brightness like snow!' exclaimed Susan.

Jenny stared at the picture and spoke quietly. 'No. It's like something else, like the purest marble.'

Mr Ligotti turned and joined the small group who were admiring the picture. Jenny heard him let out a small moan as he pushed his face closer.

This photograph was clearer than the other. Set upon a white plinth was an enormous horse's head. The mane was like foaming waves, and it fell down to the base. The ears were pointed, erect and alert, but between them was a spiralled horn which extended into a point. The teeth of the horse were as white as ice caps, but the most disturbing thing was that the eyes were also startling white, like snow-coloured glass.

'It's a unicorn,' said Jenny, almost in a whisper.

'Only the head, though,' said Sean. 'I'm afraid the rest was lost in the fire.'

Mr Ligotti looked up sharply. 'It's excellent, the finest sculpture of a horse's head I've ever seen. Your grandfather must be a truly gifted maker.' He wiped his brow and nodded; his mouth had gone dry.

Sean lowered his head. He looked across at Jenny. His glance made her feel uncomfortable.

Mr Ligotti rubbed his eyes. For a moment he seemed uncertain where he was. The storm clouds outside were clearing and the darkness was drawing back like an opening shade.

Then Mr Ligotti noticed another picture. The back of it was badly stained and Sean held it to the desktop with the tips of his fingers.

He glanced down at Sean, his eyes narrowed.

'May I?' he asked.

Sean moved his fingertips away. Mr Ligotti, with the merest hint of hesitation, picked up the picture and turned it over. He moved it nearer to his face and stepped back from the group without letting the others see it.

Susan and Jenny watched his face.

'Is this what I think . . . ?'

'Come to the fair tonight,' said Sean. Suddenly, the boy smiled for the first time as he gathered his pictures together and replaced them in his bag. 'The storm has passed.'

Gently, he took the picture from Mr Ligotti's fingers.

'I think that's enough for today,' said Mr Ligotti, almost to himself.

Jenny and Susan had been round the common twice. There was a good turnout of people from the town and they saw several of their friends from school, plus some of their teachers, along with their own children. The atmosphere was intoxicating and they loved it. They greedily drank in the swirling colour as if it were a magical potion. The air was a sweet mixture of candy floss and toffee apples. Cries and shouts of laughter were swept up into the night sky. The fairground organ music rang out above the heads of the crowd and rattled away like a delirious, demonic anthem.

'I'm giddy from it all!' said Susan at last, as she fell back against a white picket fence, which surrounded a speedway ride.

Jenny laughed and leant beside her. She gave a snort and once again peered across the fair, into the multi-coloured loops of lights beside the row of sideshow attractions.

'You're still looking for him, aren't you?' said Susan after a moment.

Jenny did not reply. She was searching out faces amongst the sideshow barkers, cajoling and hurrying people along.

'We haven't looked at the far end of the fair yet,' she said. 'Perhaps his grandfather's show is there?'

Suddenly, Susan grabbed Jenny by the arm and held it tight.

'Look,' she hissed.

'Where?'

Susan nodded towards a pair of figures who were standing in the shadow of the big wheel: a tall man in a black overcoat who stood beside a smaller boy.

'I don't believe it! That's Mr Ligotti!'

'And . . . and he's with Sean!' The two girls gawped at one another.

'I wonder what they're up to?' said Susan.

'I bet Mr Ligotti's come to have a look at those models—Sean did say "come to the fair" didn't he?'

The two figures stood talking for only a few seconds longer, and then began to make their way along a track that led to the showmen's caravans.

Jenny tugged at her friend's arm. 'Come on, let's follow them. Perhaps we can see too?'

Reluctantly, Susan allowed Jenny to pull her along with her. They kept a safe distance between themselves and the pair ahead, bobbing in and out of the dark spots afforded by the shelter of the caravans. Finally, up ahead, Sean and Mr Ligotti stopped in front of a large chrome trailer.

They watched as Sean opened the door with a key which hung from a neck-chain. As the door opened, shadows yawned. The two girls crept closer so that they could hear.

'I set it out earlier for you,' said Sean's voice. 'I knew you'd come.'

Mr Ligotti stepped up into the trailer and Sean closed the door behind them. The girls continued to watch as an amber light suddenly glowed from inside the trailer. The single net-curtained window shimmered as they saw shapes move within.

'I bet he's showing him the unicorn head. Let's move closer,' said Jenny. 'Perhaps we can get to see too.'

Susan stood her ground. 'No,' she said; a tinge of fear suddenly edged her voice. 'I don't think I want to.'

'Stay there then, I'm going to knock.'

Susan reached out to grab her friend's arm, but Jenny had gone.

Slowly, she edged her way towards the trailer.

Suddenly, they heard it. It was a cry—almost certainly human—but it was strangled and twisted. The trailer door burst open and Mr Ligotti stood on the top steps. He cried out again then leapt down.

'*Il mostro!*' he cried as he staggered forward. He looked without seeing as he turned his face towards Jenny. 'It is not possible, not possible. But you see—I touched it.'

Quickly, he crossed himself and ran past the two girls into the night.

Jenny turned to look back at Susan who held her hands to her face.

'Mr Ligotti!'

Jenny turned around. Sean stood in the doorway; his fingers nervously tussled with his hair.

'But he wanted to see!' said the boy. 'He needed to know! Isn't that what the lesson was about?'

He stepped back and gestured to Jenny to step up into the trailer. For a moment she glanced back at her friend who was still transfixed.

Slowly, carefully, she took the first step and then a second.

Sean turned and led her into the trailer. The room was imbued with a warm glow from a single gas lamp. Ahead, just to the right, was a table, on which something lay partly covered beneath a white sheet. Slowly, he pulled the cover away. Jenny's mouth dried. He struck a match and lit another small lamp just behind the table.

The object's head became back-lit. Part of it seemed to have been damaged—it was only just possible to make out a face—but it was the softest, most serene face Jenny thought she had ever seen. After a moment she realized that it seemed to be the remains of a sculpture or model of a person.

'What is it?' she whispered.

'Isn't it obvious?' said Sean with a smile. 'Look.'

He pulled the sheet further back.

Jenny's bottom lip trembled as she saw the two wings and the snow-white feathers. They were dishevelled but grand and they arrived at two large arched points—just as she had seen in pictures and in church windows.

'Go on,' urged Sean, a crescent grin spread beneath his fringe. 'Touch him if you'd like.'

'It's beautiful, better than in pictures, fantastic . . . What is it made of . . . ?' she trailed off.

She heard the voice of Melanie in her head, the girl in her class with the round spectacles, she had asked Mr Ligotti a question.

'*Do angels exist, sir?*'

She hesitated for a moment, then reached out to touch the face. There was a sudden crash.

'You darn young fool!'

Jenny turned with a cry. A wild-eyed man with a beard stood in the doorway of the caravan behind them. For a moment he was simply a shape.

'What have you done, Sean? Get her away, now!'

'It's my gramps,' said Sean. 'You'd better go.'

'You fool,' said the man to Sean, as she leapt from the caravan.

Jenny ran from the place, past Susan who followed her, neither stopping to look behind them. They ran and ran, leaving the fairground and its lights and its smells far behind.

The new teacher, Miss Bunce, was introduced by the Head.

'Class, I know that some of you were worried about Sean. This is Miss Bunce, who I think some of you may know. She's taking the class whilst Mr Ligotti is away sick . . . Miss Bunce has made some enquiries about Sean.'

He made a gesture to the young woman.

'It's just to say that Sean is quite safe. We have word that he and his grandfather have moved on to another funfair somewhere—but . . . well, we don't know where.'

A murmur rose from the class.

'He was an interesting boy,' said the Head.

'His grandfather was a great model maker,' said Jenny. 'We saw some of his pictures, of his work.'

Susan smiled at Jenny.

Miss Bunce laughed. 'How marvellous. They were an extraordinary family. Went back years. They had travelled the world, been to strange places, seen everything—amazing things.'

The Head smiled and made to leave. Just as he reached the door, Miss Bunce suddenly raised her finger to her lip.

'Oh, just one thing.'

Jenny looked up.

'His grandfather wasn't a model maker. Oh no. One of the fairhands told me. He . . . well, how can I put this? He treated dead things, stuffed them—you know, he was a taxidermist. Very good apparently.'

Susan reached out and squeezed Jenny's hand. Jenny just stared ahead of her, aware only of a ringing in her ears. Her hand was as cold as ice.

At home, Mr Ligotti lay silently in a darkened room, remembering Rome and thinking of Mysteries.

[illegible]

[illegible]

[illegible]

[illegible] collection, reprinted by permission of The [illegible]

[illegible] in this [illegible] of Conville and Walsh [illegible] on behalf of the author.

Acknowledgements

'The Adventure of the Dented Computer' © Simon Cheshire, 2003. First published in this collection; reproduced by permission of The Agency (London) Ltd on behalf of the author.
'Rodier's Necklace' © Linda Newbery, 2003, first published in this collection by permission of The Maggie Noach Literary Agency on behalf of the author.
'Bad Presents' © David Belbin, 2003, first published in this collection by permission of Jennifer Luithlen Agency on behalf of the author.
'Gone Away' © John Gordon, 2003, first published in this collection by permission of the author.
'Yesterday Upon the Stair' © Dennis Hamley, 2003, first published in this collection by permission of the author.
'Double Rap' © Hilary McKay, 2003, first published in this collection by permission of Jennifer Luithlen Agency on behalf of the author.
'Maggie's Window' © Marjorie Darke, 2003, first published in this collection by permission of the author c/o Rogers, Coleridge and White Ltd.
'Earth 23' © Robert Dawson, 2003, first published in this collection by permission of Pollinger Ltd on behalf of the author.
'The Happy Alien' © Jean Ure, 2003, first published in this collection by permission of The Maggie Noach Literary Agency on behalf of the author.
'The Drowning' © Malcolm Rose, 2003, first published in this collection by permission of Juvenilia on behalf of the author.
'Bad Dreams' © Douglas Hill, 2003, first published in this collection by permission of Watson, Little Ltd on behalf of the author.
'Sarah' © Alison Prince, 2003, first published in this collection by permission of Jennifer Luithlen Agency on behalf of the author.
'Doing the Bank' © Jan Burchett and Sara Vogler, 2003. First published in this collection; reproduced by permission of The Agency (London) Ltd on behalf of the authors.
'Mysteries' © Laurence Staig, 2003, first published in this collection by permission of Conville and Walsh Ltd on behalf of the author.